Finding True Love at 35,000 Feet

THE SAGA OF EMMA AND JOHN

By George S. Naas

Golden Publishing Company – Lakewood, CO
in collaboration with TWB Press – Lakewood, CO
2019

Edited and formatted for publication by Terry Wright at TWB Press – www.twbpress.com

Published by
Golden Publishing Company, Inc.
PO Box 150425
Lakewood, CO 80215
USA

ISBN: 9780970714268

Finding True Love at 35,000 Feet

ON A WARM SUMMER NIGHT at Athens International Airport, a travel-weary Captain John Peterson of the Unites States Army Airborne Rangers (the most elite fighting force in the armed forces) sat quietly, eating a Big Mac and washing it down with a Coke. His mind was far from the battlefield he had left in Afghanistan just seven hours earlier. He was on his way home to Denver, Colorado. John's third and last tour of duty was over, and soon his army career would also be over. Even though the war was now a long ways away, thirty-year-old John glanced around the room at the people, wary of any threats. His gaze went from one person to the next and stopped and went back to the last woman he had looked at, and there it stayed.

Emma Mansfield, a twenty-nine-year-old Doctor of Optometry, looked back at him while she spooned chocolate ice cream out of a paper cup. As she slowly pulled the spoon past her rose red lips, she thought: he is gorgeous and sure fills out that uniform nicely. He must have a six pack. She watched him put on his dark-framed glasses. Oh well, he's probably not going to Denver. He's probably married or engaged, at least, as he's too good looking to be on the market.

John thought: I hope to God she's going to Denver—but that

would be a long-shot so I better forget it. Goddamn, she is absolutely beautiful. Hell, she probably has a husband or a boyfriend. If she does, he must be a dumbass not to be here with her.

Both of their trains of thought were interrupted by a voice on the intercom announcing that Delta flight 221 to Chicago would be boarding at Gate 22A at 10:45pm. Emma and John waited to see which one would get up first. Emma stood and smiled at him then walked down the concourse toward 22A, dragging her purple carry-on with a yellow ribbon tied on the handle.

Trailing several feet behind her, John did some multitasking. He studied everything about her, the way she walked and carried her purse, all the time thinking: please, please stop at Gate 22A.

His heart sank as she walked past it but was relieved when he realized she was just going to the ladies restroom. He leaned up against a post, all the while never taking his eyes off the restroom doorway. Someone tapped him on his shoulder. He turned and saw a couple in their seventies standing there with big smiles on their faces.

"We want to thank you for your service to our wonderful country."

"Sure. You're welcome. Good to talk to you."

The old man said, "I was in the army myself, son, only that was a long time back. I wish I could be in the army now. I would love to be over there fighting those godforsaken heathens."

John muttered, "No, you wouldn't."

Emma combed her long brown hair and fixed her lipstick but

could not get the handsome soldier out of her mind. As she strolled out of the restroom, she saw him talking to the old couple, and not wanting to disturb their conversation, she ignored them made her way to the plane and seat 19B.

In the time it took John to finish with the old couple, he had missed seeing the beautiful woman come out of the ladies room. He leaned up against the post again, waiting until the last call to board Flight 221.

Now with a confused look on his face, he walked down the walkway and, after looking around for her in vain, made his way to seat 3A. He sat there staring out the window and watching the last of the baggage being loaded on the plane. Then he saw it, the purple carry-on with a yellow ribbon tied on the handle. It was hers. He remembered how she had pulled it along with her when she went to the ladies bathroom. He thought she must've had to check it because the overhead racks were full.

Just as soon as the plane was airborne and the seatbelt sign had gone off, he made his way down the aisle, looking to the right and left. Passing rows 17 and 18, he saw her sitting in 19B. There was a nineteen-year-old kid sitting in 19A. Looking at her, and then the kid, John said, "Hey, 19A, you want to trade your seat for a first class one and get a couple hundred bucks thrown in for good measure?"

The skinny young man said, "Make it $500 and you got a deal."

John pulled out five one-hundred-dollar bills, and reaching past the woman, he delivered the cash. "Done."

As a very happy kid squeezed past the woman, John smiled at her. "You want the window seat now, or do you want me to sit there?"

Emma replied, laughingly, "I don't know. Maybe, I should sell you my seat and move up to where Larry is sitting."

"Who is Larry?"

"He is the guy you just paid five hundred dollars to give up a seat next to me."

"Well, I was hoping you would stay here so I can get to know you."

Smiling, she said, "That would depend on just how well you want to get to know me. I suppose my choice of seat would weigh to some extent on my decision since, depending on your intentions, I could find myself trapped between the window and you. Whereas if I stay in 19B, you would be by the window and I could get up and run for help if necessary."

"I promise you that you won't have to cry for help."

"Well, you do look nice, and I remember you from McDonald's. So, I guess I'll move over."

Holding out his right hand as he sat down, he said, "John Peterson, soon to be just another US citizen."

"Emma Peterson." Quickly correcting herself, she said, "I mean Emma Mansfield."

"Sounds like a Freudian slip to me." Looking into her beautiful brown eyes, he smiled. "So what does Emma Mansfield Peterson do for a living? And please don't tell me you have a husband and three kids."

"Actually, I'm single and I have a younger sister and I live in Boulder, Colorado, and I'm a Doctor of Optometry and I have my own practice in Boulder. If you're wondering how old I am, I'm twenty-nine. So what about you, John Peterson?"

"I turned the terrible age of thirty last week. I was the commanding officer of Charlie Company, but not anymore because our 365 on the line in Afghanistan is over, and we're all going home. In my case that's Denver. My platoon leaders got me a cake for my birthday, but the Taliban got lucky and dropped a mortar round a little too close to us and got shrapnel in my cake. We ate what we could after picking out the pieces of metal."

Emma put her hand on his bare forearm and looked into his eyes. "You *are* joking, aren't you?"

"Afghanistan isn't like what you see on the nightly news. During my first two tours, I had to write four letters of condolence to the families of the Rangers that I lost. This time, thank God, I didn't have to write a single one." John pointed to the glasses on his face. "My frames are getting a little loose. Maybe I can come to your place and get a new pair when we get back home."

"Let's see what the problem is now."

Before John could take them off, Emma, with her face no more than five inches from his, gently took off his glasses and examined them.

John thought: I blew it! She was so close to me, I should have kissed her. God! I'm stupid sometimes.

Emma studied the frames. "Part of the problem is the screw that holds the earpiece to the rest of the frame. It's loose on the right side. I can fix it right now."

"How?"

"I have a small screwdriver in my purse."

"You carry around a screwdriver?"

"Of course!" She took out the tiny screwdriver and tightened the errant screw. "You didn't ask me what I was doing in this part of the world. I work one month each year with Doctors without Borders. We go to poor countries and help people who have never seen a doctor in their lives." Rubbing her finger on the side of the right earpiece, she noticed a gray mark on the frame. "Do you know what caused this?"

"Sure do."

"What is it?"

"About a month ago, me and some of my men from third platoon were working in conjunction with the Afghanistan National Army, checking out a small village. We thought the village was free of the Taliban because little kids were running around playing and coming up to my men. There was one Taliban soldier in the town, hiding behind a dirt wall. As we came around a corner with a bunch of kids running alongside us, he stepped out in the street and opened up on us. He killed two Afghanistan soldiers and three kids. His last round was meant for me, but his aim was off just far enough to only graze my glasses and knock them off. He was out of bullets. I wasn't. I lit him up. He won't be killing anybody else for Allah."

Touching the top of his bare arm, she said softly, "You talk about dying as if it's just a normal way of life. Aren't you scared when you go out on these patrols?"

"Sure. At least I was at first, but then I got used to it. Getting back to my glasses, though, do you think they'll fit better now?"

"Let's see."

John watched Emma take a small towel from her purse and clean the lenses. He noticed her dainty hands and her fingernails painted with the same color polish as her lipstick.

She twisted sideways in her seat. "Okay, hold your head up."

He did as he was told, his own body turned toward her, his heart skipping around like a kid on a playground.

She gently pushed the glasses up to his face and checked to see how they fit behind his ears. Now within four inches of his face to see how he looked, she didn't object as John put his right hand behind her head and pulled her lips toward his. They kissed each other with passion and tenderness. She put both of her hands on his bare biceps and squeezed. His arms felt as if they were made of steel. Their passionate kissing continued for a good two minutes and provided a sideshow for some of the passengers sitting in close proximity.

It was only broken up when the flight attendant cleared her

throat. "Do you lovebirds want anything to drink with the dinner we'll be serving shortly?"

John straightened in his seat. "Sure. A Coke would be okay."

Emma, acting as if nothing had happened, opted for a glass of iced tea and then said to John, "Do you think that was a good idea?"

With a sparkle in his eyes and a grin on his face he kissed her again. "I don't know. I don't drink iced tea."

"You know what I mean...the kiss...we just met—"

"Yes." John answered. "It was a great idea, and we still have ten hours of kissing to go."

Emma, using a tissue, carefully wiped her lipstick off John's mouth. "Then what?"

John kissed her hand. "I don't want this to end at Denver International. Do you?"

"I guess we'll have to wait and see how we feel when we land, see what our feelings lead to."

"I know what I want them to lead to." John grinned.

Emma took hold of his hand and rubbed his knuckles with her thumb then whispered in his ear, "I know exactly what you want."

He took hold of her hand and pressed his palm against hers. "Be careful or you might make another one of those Freudian slips." Moving his face closer to hers, he then moved in to kiss her again but the flight attendant interrupted with the drinks, quickly followed by their dinners.

As Emma ate a vegan meal of vegetables, John had a blood-red steak and potatoes.

She poked his steak with her fork. "How can you eat that? It looks like they never even cooked it?"

"Well, because I'm hungry and I like my steak medium rare."

"That one is still mooing."

"So, Emma, it just dawned on me. Where did you fly from? I'm guessing that you were not working in Greece."

"Right. Madagascar. I worked with patients who contracted Rift Valley Fever, which spread into Hemorrhagic Fever, Encephalitis, and then ocular diseases. It's spread by person-to-person contact." Laughing, she added, "I hope you haven't kissed anyone lately who has been in the Androy region of Madagascar. You could be in big trouble."

John leaned over to kiss her again. "I'll take my chances."

As his hand closed in on her right breast, she intercepted it and held his hand to her forehead. "Do I feel hot?"

"Oh, I hope so," he breathed.

"On the off chance we keep seeing each other in Denver, I want to know more about you, and don't lie."

"I never lie. Ask my men."

"That won't do any good. I don't think you're planning on going out on a date with any of them."

Gently putting his hand on her shoulder, he looked into her beautiful brown eyes, hoping she'd understand his sincerity. "I would never lie to you."

She stared back at him, mute.

For a few seconds, he said nothing then blurted out, "My boys in Charlie Company refer to me as a hard-case because I lead. I was never in the rear with the gear, letting someone else put his butt on the line in my place. I would have died for any one of my men, and they knew it, and any one of them would have died for me. I already said four of my Rangers did die for me. Maybe, if I had planned our assaults better on two different engagements during my first two tours of fighting, they wouldn't be buried in Arlington. This is a guilt I now have to live with for the rest of my life. I console myself thinking that someday, when I buy the farm, I'll walk into Big Daddy's Bar and Grill, and they'll be waiting for me. I hope so because that will mean that I made it to Heaven somehow. On the other hand, if a kid we all referred to as *Ace* said, 'Captain, they're fresh out of Berliner Weisse. It looks like you'll have to settle for a Bud Light.' Then I'll know that I'd gone to hell with the twenty-two Taliban insurgents I personally sent there. Now, if you'll excuse me..."

As John got up to use the restroom, it gave Emma time to think. I feel safe being with John and I know he would take care of me, and I think I'm falling in love with him. This is all so confusing. What's the matter with me? I only met him a few hours ago! I'll cool it on the kissing...although it was wonderful. If I don't, what'is he going to think of me? I'm sure he has been with plenty of women. I don't want him to think that I'm going to be up for a one-night stand with him anytime in the near future. It's going to be platonic from now on, all the way to Denver. I do want to date him in Denver, though. This is another good reason to not give in and let him have what I know he wants. He's going to have to wait for that. When he gets back, I'll ask him about his family and girlfriends—but I won't be too pushy.

While John washed his face, he was thinking of Emma. He thought kissing her soft lips was great, and that perfume she wore added to her beautiful face and body—that slim and sexy body and perfect breasts. I've never been with a woman like her in my life. I better be careful though. It could turn her off if she were to think all I wanted to do was bed her, which I would love to do. It's a pleasure to be with a woman who isn't just beautiful but intelligent as well. I can't come on too strong, but I can't let her think I'm some pussy that'll worship her. I just hope we can develop a relationship in Denver. I think she really likes me. I hope she doesn't have some guy in Denver that she has been dating. Maybe she is so wrapped up in her job that she doesn't have time for a boyfriend. I hope that is the case. She acts as if she doesn't mind my being in the Army, for now anyway.

John came back and sat down, and as he did she said, "You got some water on your shirt."

"Good thing it isn't food or a drink. It'll dry. All my gear is being taken to Fort Carson by a friend, the officer of my first platoon. I could have taken a military transport but I would have had to wait another three days. I didn't want to wait. I've seen enough of Iraq and Afghanistan to last me a lifetime."

Stretching in her seat with her arms over her head she said to John, "Tell me something about your family."

John didn't fail to notice how stretching made her breasts press out more from her dress. "Tell me about your family first."

"I have a Mom and Dad who live in Boulder, and a sister, Jane, who is twenty-seven, married, and Mom to a six-year-old daughter named Maggie. Her husband, Larry Miller, is a really good guy. He's an engineer for Martin. Your turn, John."

"I had a girlfriend but she cheated on me during my second tour. I came back early and wanted to surprise her but the surprise was on me. She opened the door and was obviously several months pregnant. It was then that I knew why she wanted me to make her the beneficiary on my life insurance. I guess she was hoping that I would get lit up. Then she and the lowlife she was living with could collect the twenty-five grand payout."

"That's awful! I didn't know a woman could be that cold."

"I was bummed out for a few months, but the war has a way of putting things in perspective. As Corporal Felix Garcia (God rest his soul) used to say: "Bad beginnings can have happy endings. I guess he was right. If I were still with Mary Ann, I would have never met you, and that would've been a tragedy."

"You would've met someone else."

John put his arm around Emma. "True enough. But would you

have thought it was a tragedy if you had never met me? Be honest."

"Yes."

"So, Emma, did you have a relationship with some guy?"

"How do you know I don't have one now?"

"Well, assuming you don't mean me, you couldn't have a boyfriend now or you wouldn't have let me kiss you, and you wouldn't have kissed me back. Am I right?"

"I had a guy-friend for about a month, but I quit talking to him when he became too possessive."

"How bad was too possessive?"

"Brad always wanted to know where I was going, and he didn't like me doing things with my friends. He would park in front of my home and confront me as to where I had been when I came home and got out of my car. One day he grabbed my arm and twisted it...left a bruise on my forearm. That was the last straw. I told him I'd call the police if he ever showed his face around me again. He now sends me emails, wanting to know how many times I've slept with someone and what nasty things I did with him. I never slept with Brad. I think that's what got under his skin."

"I would love to meet Brad."

"He likes to think he is mister macho."

"Emma, when we get to Denver, maybe you wouldn't mind introducing me to Brad. I think I can convince him to leave you alone. Besides, if things go well between us, maybe you'll think of yourself as my girl."

"What will you think of me?"

"My girlfriend and maybe a considerable lot more, depending as to how things work out."

"John, enough about Brad. Do you believe in God?" Emma laid her head on his shoulder and waited for his answer.

It was a few seconds in coming since he had to think about it. "Sometimes I do and sometimes I don't. When I see what's going on in the world, it makes me wonder what God is doing. We were walking down the Highway to Hell a couple of months ago and ran across a burned-out school bus. Inside the bus, we found the charred bodies of twelve kids. I don't know why God let that happen. Maybe he was busy and didn't notice what was going on. The Bible says, "Vengeance is mine, saith the Lord."

"Since God was too busy to carry out his vengeance, my Rangers decided to help him out. We surprised fifteen Taliban insurgents about a mile down the road. They were taking turns raping five school girls that they had taken off the bus. They gave up without a fight. While I was gone to Regimental to report on what had happened, a Humvee came and picked up the girls. My men then executed all fifteen Taliban rapists and murderers. They shot all of them and poured gas on them and dropped in a match and watched them burn. When I came back, we left our death cards on their corpses. We later got a call from Alpha 2-5. They wanted to know where to pick up the prisoners. 'What prisoners?' I asked. They knew what we did. We were never asked about them again. This was just another day on the line in Afghanistan. So you see, God helps those who help themselves. I hope that answers your question."

"What are death cards?"

"It's a regular deck of playing cards but on the back of each card is our Ranger logo and the words: Charlie 2-5."

"Why would you do that? They'd know who killed their men, and they'd come looking for you!"

"Exactly! That's the whole idea. We wanted them to come after us. It makes it easier to kill them. The Taliban are really bad soldiers. They're mainly ignorant and illiterate men in their thirties who are in poor physical shape. No Ranger has ever lost a fight in hand-to-hand combat with them. I can break one of them in half, just like a twig on a bush."

Emma thought: I guess he did what he had to do. War has given John a hard side, out of necessity, but I've seen his soft side too. He can be sweet and he knows what he wants and I think he wants me. I love his smile and it turns me on knowing I'm with a real man.

"So, tell me about what you did before joining the Army."

"I lived in Lakewood all my life. My parents, Edward and Ann, still live in the same house that my sister, Ellen, and I were raised in. We all went to church every Sunday. However, whatever Methodist religion I retained had vanished in Afghanistan."

"And school?" She blinked.

"I graduated from Lakewood High and wanted to serve our

country. I was accepted to West Point. After graduating 47th in my class, I was sent to Fort Benning, Georgia, for Airborne and Ranger Training. After A R T, I was assigned to the 75th Ranger Regiment and was deployed to Iraq as a Second Lieutenant. I was promoted to First Lieutenant when First Lieutenant Harry Nicholes was killed in action. I was promoted to Captain after an IUD wounded our CO, and he was sent back to the states."

John looked at Emma and saw that she was fast asleep. He thought as he gently pushed her hair back, God she is beautiful, even while asleep. He looked down at the perfect curves of her body and her slim and graceful legs. He longed to see the rest of her but knew it might take a while to get to do that. He leaned his head over where it touched the top of Emma's. Her hair smells good, he thought and then fell asleep.

About two hours out of Chicago, both Emma and John woke up at the same time. Emma looked up at him and smiled. "Now you can't say we've never slept together."

John sat up in his seat. "I told you my entire life story and you went to sleep in the middle of it. I must be boring as hell."

"I'm sorry. I was just so tired. I'll make it up to you. We still have some time to go before we get to O'Hare."

"Okay, Emma, now it's your turn. I promise I won't go to sleep."

"Well, let's see. I was raised a Catholic and I still go to mass every Sunday in Boulder at Sacred Heart of Jesus Catholic Church. I especially like Father William Pierce. He has a way of speaking to you as if he has known you forever, even if he's just met you. I've helped him with some of our poorer parishioners by giving them free eye exams and glasses. Oh, my parents and sister and her family are church members, too. My sister was married there. I hope to get married there someday."

"Not to Brad, though."

"Definitely not to Brad."

With that cute smile that Emma liked, John said, "Got anyone in mind?"

Glancing at John, Emma remarked, "Not quite yet, but I'm working on it."

"Do you like your job?"

"I love my job and the fact that I have my own practice."

He leaned back in his seat. "I guess it must pay pretty good."

"I make a very good living, thank you very much."

"Don't get mad. I was just asking. Once I get out of the Army I might be looking for a woman to take care of me." Laughing out loud he added, "We're on the opposite ends of the spectrum. You help people and they pay you and I kill people and the government pays me."

Their conversation was cut short by an announcement from the Captain. "For all of you who are going to Denver on Delta 191 that was scheduled to leave at 10:47, I'm sorry to say that the flight has been cancelled due to a mechanical problem. Delta Air Lines is sorry for this inconvenience. Since 191 was the last flight out to Denver tonight, Delta will pay for a room at the Airport Chicago Hilton for all Denver-bound passengers. The next available flight out will be tomorrow morning at 11:55. You'll have priority seating on that flight, which is Delta 222. We show that only seven people on this flight were scheduled to fly on Delta 191. Once again, Delta Air Lines is sorry for the inconvenience."

"Darn it," Emma said.

John was secretly delighted. "Well, we'll just have to make the best of it."

She stared at him with a suspicious look. "I know what you're thinking. But forget it. Delta is paying for two rooms. They didn't say anything about us bunking together."

With a phony look of shock on his face, he said, "That never crossed my mind."

"Yes it did, and you're still thinking about it. You know how you told me that you never lie? Well, you just did."

"I was thinking about my guys coming home to their families, wives, and girlfriends, and I was hoping you'd go with me to our welcome home celebration at Fort Carson in three days. There'll be the local TV people covering our return. It'd be nice if you were there with me. We could call it our first date in Colorado."

"Okay, I'll go. But quit lying about what's really on your mind when we land."

"Now that's enough of that. You keep bringing it up, so it

seems to me that sex is all *you* are thinking about."

"Maybe I thought about it a little." She shrugged.

"I'll tell you what we can do once we get through customs and get our hotel room."

"Rooms."

"I know Chicago really well so we can go out to dinner and then take the Lake Front Path down by Lake Michigan. It's really pretty and romantic, and it would be great strolling along with the prettiest girl in Illinois...and Colorado. After that we could top the night off at Paps Ultimate Bar and Grill. They have karaoke and they're right next to our hotel. We'll have a blast. Do you like karaoke?"

"Yes."

"Then we go to our separate rooms and meet up for breakfast. What do you think? Do you trust me?"

"Yes, but I know what you're still hoping for."

"Okay, you're kind of right."

Putting her hands up to his face and squeezing his cheeks together, she said, "And you are still kind of lying."

With that, she gave him a kiss on his forehead. "You're kind of cute, and I sing karaoke really well."

"So do I, Emma. So do I."

They then proceeded to discuss all the music that they liked, settling on two songs that they both liked: *Thinking out Loud* and *All of Me.*

The Captain came on again. "We've begun our final descent to O'Hare International Airport where the temperature is a balmy 78 degrees. As your Captain, I want to thank you for flying Delta Airlines, and we hope to see you again in the future. We should be on the ground in about eighteen minutes."

After that announcement, John took Emma's hand and they looked out into the darkness at the Skyline of Chicago and started singing *All of Me* softly to each other over the sound of the jet engines.

***

Getting in line to go through customs, Emma said, "Look at those lines. There must be five hundred people waiting, and they are just crawling."

"I can fix it so we can get through customs in five minutes."

"How?"

Picking up her suitcase in his left hand and taking hold of her left hand with his right, he said, "Lift up the rope and walk under it."

As she did, she looked confused. "Are we going to cut the line?"

"No, don't need to." As he pulled her along at a fast rate, with Emma trying to run in high heels, John said, "What does that sign say?"

"United States Military Personnel."

"They'll wave me right on through. You say that you are my

fiancée, and they'll look at your passport for about ten seconds and say welcome back to the U.S."

A nervous Emma handed her passport to the female customs agent who looked at it for ten seconds and said, "Welcome home. When are you two getting married?"

John answered, "Three weeks from today, aren't we, sweetie?"

"That's right, darling."

John grabbed Emma as she said, "Thank you" to the customs agent and gave her one passionate kiss. She put her left hand on his shoulder, and the other hand held her passport down to her side.

The customs agent thought: God, they look like they are truly in love. I hope it lasts a lifetime for them.

As they walked out into the Chicago night, John bragged, "See, kid, rank has its privileges."

"You have me convinced. Now what?"

"We get our hotel room and then go out on the town."

"You mean we get our two rooms and then go out on the town."

"I thought that's what I said."

"You thought wrong."

"Are you sure?"

"Yes. You've said only one room twice now, John. Don't give me that innocent look."

"My God, Emma, you have a one-track mind."

***

Walking up to the counter at the Hilton, John said to the clerk, "You have two reservations for Captain John Peterson and Emma Mansfield courtesy of Delta Air Lines."

The clerk said, "Yes. Here they are. We have two adjoining rooms or one single on the ninth floor and the other single on the seventh floor."

Before Emma could say a word, John quickly spoke up. "We want the two adjoining rooms."

The clerk said, "We have 918 and 919. Do either of you have a preference?"

A slightly annoyed Emma said, "I don't, as long as the adjoining doors can be locked from my side."

"Of course they can," the bewildered clerk replied. "I thought the two of you were together. I'm sorry. Here are your keys."

As they took the elevator to the ninth floor, John looked at Emma who had her arms folded and was looking straight ahead. He tried to make small talk with her. "Nice place, huh?"

"Yes, John. It *is* a nice place."

Getting off the elevator, John carried Emma's suitcase and waited while she unlocked the door to her room.

Going inside, he put her suitcase on a table and checked the adjoining door to make sure it was locked. "Emma, if you'd feel better I'll go back down and get one of the other single rooms. And if those are taken, since the place is pretty booked up, I'll sleep in the lobby tonight, when we get back from going out. I'm really looking forward to our first official date."

Seeing the forlorn look on his face, Emma said, "Come here. I like the thought of you being in the next room. If somebody were to break into my room, who better to protect me than a very cute and well-built Captain John Peterson of the U.S. Army Rangers?" Slipping her arms around him, she leaned up and kissed him.

"I wish I had a change of uniform. This one's all wrinkled from hours on a plane."

"Let me iron it for you." She pointed to a wall-mounted iron. "Complimentary."

"There's probably one in my room. I can do it."

"What's the fun in that? Open the door on your side and I'll open my side, and then you can hand me your pants and shirt. I'll change into a fresh dress while you're getting undressed."

John, who was more use to issuing orders than receiving them, was more than happy to say, "Yes ma'am," as he saluted Emma.

She saluted him back.

He chuckled as he looked at her sweet face. "Emma, FYI this time. You always salute with your right hand, not your left."

After getting into his room, he took off his uniform, and wearing only his tan military boxer shorts, he went over and knocked on his side of Emma's door.

She opened the door, her face turned away. "Just hand them to me. I won't look."

"I still have my military boxer shorts on. They're no different than swim trunks."

Emma was glad to turn around, though she would not admit it to John. She longed to see him without his shirt on. Everything about his body was pure muscles. He had the mandatory military six-pack. Now Emma was the one being careful not to come on to him too much. "Come in. We can talk while I iron your clothes."

He sat in a plush chair.

She noticed he had a four-inch scar above his left knee. "What caused that?"

"A Diadem."

She threw him a questioning look.

"It's a snake that's found in Iraq and Afghanistan. During my second deployment, we were pinned down by enemy fire. I felt a sharp pain in my leg and thought I'd been hit with an enemy round. I knew an AK bullet coming straight at me would've gone right through me and kept on going, so I assumed it had ricocheted. Then I saw the snake slithering off. Corporal Charlie Mantella, our medic, crawled over and cut my fatigues and made a slice in my leg, which made it bleed like hell, but he saved my life. It's as good as new now."

"John, how can you stand going through that hell without going crazy?"

"Well, I like to think that I was fighting for my country and my family, but now that I've met you, I would take on the devil himself to protect you."

Emma thought: I think he really loves me, but am I falling in love with him? I've never been with anyone like him. Mrs. John Peterson—I like the way that sounds. I guess I'll have to see what develops.

John watched Emma iron his Ranger uniform. He thought how gorgeous she looked, even with her back turned to him. Wearing a purple dress and shoes just a shade lighter than the dress, she turned around and smiled. "Here you are. All done."

"Thanks." He climbed into the trousers. "I don't even have a comb for my hair." Before he could put on his shirt, she pushed him back down into the chair.

"Allow me." She got out a comb from her suitcase and proceeded to comb his hair. "John, do you like Mexican food?"

"I love Mexican food."

"Then why don't we go to the restaurant in the hotel. I think the name is El Gordos."

"It sounds fine to me."

***

Walking hand-in-hand into El Gordos, John glanced at Emma. "Mexican food is the one food I couldn't get in Afghanistan."

"Why is that?"

"Well, rumor was our commanding general didn't like it, so no one was allowed to eat it."

"That wasn't very nice of him."

"I don't think it bothered him a whole lot. This is all in the past for me now. In forty-five days I'll be a civilian, and so will First Lieutenant Larry Peoples and Second Lieutenant Nathan Gee. We are going to start a security business with Sergeant Major Tennyson Henry. We think there's a need for providing security to big businesses, especially in the times in which we live."

Sitting in a small booth side-by-side with their legs touching made John think that paradise was right next to him, his for the asking. But she would make him work for it, of that he was sure.

Emma broke into his train of thought. "John..." She sucked margarita through a straw. "What do you think I want in life?"

"I thought you already have what you want."

"More than just my practice, I want a husband and a couple of kids, and then I'll consider my life perfect. My mother is always bugging me to get married. She likes to remind me that my biological clock is ticking, so I had better hurry up. She thinks that if she keeps pushing me I'll finally settle for just anyone. Jane fixed me up with a guy that works with her husband. He wasn't bad looking, and he was smart but really boring."

"Maybe your mother will like me."

"She would if you lied and told her that you were Catholic. You couldn't do that because you never lie...or so you say."

"Is being Catholic a high priority to you or just your mom?"

Holding her thought, Emma took timeout to order her dinner. "I'll have a bean tostada and a vegan tamale."

John ordered as if he were commanding his troops. "Give me the chicken, steak, and shrimp fajitas. Smother them in green chili. I don't want any cheese, bell peppers, sour cream, or guacamole. Nix all of that stuff and make the steak rare."

Putting her drink down, Emma told the waiter, "I'll take his guacamole."

As the waiter left to turn in their order, John pushed up closer to Emma and rubbed her back. "Why would you want to eat something that looks like frog guts?"

"Well, mister know-it-all, for starters, guacamole is rich in vitamin K, which is vital in blood clotting. It could come in handy in case you plan on being shot in the future. If you move your hand down any farther, I may shoot you myself."

Moving his hand back up to her shoulder, he whined, "Sorry, I wasn't trying to put the make on you."

"Yes you were. Right where your hand is, that's fine. Just don't plan on going cross-country with it again."

As Emma went back to talking about the advantages of guacamole and looking at John and saying how it was good for eye health, especially in small children, John was thinking of something else. God her breasts have got to be just beautiful and sexy beyond belief. Maybe she will be kind and let me see them before the night is over. Tuning her conversation back in, he heard her say, "So that's why guacamole is a good food source."

After finishing off their dinner, they took a cab down to the

Chicago Lakefront Path. The view of Chicago was spectacular and the warm breeze coming off Lake Michigan blew Emma's long brown hair back and forth, causing her to continually rearrange it. They walked hand-in-hand. Emma was thinking: maybe he brought me here to make me fall in love with him. If that's what he's thinking, he's not going to have to try very hard. I think I've already fallen in love with him.

They sat in the sand at a dog beach, but at 11:27pm, no dogs were around. There was, though, a suspicious man following them. He had gone unnoticed to Emma but not to John.

Looking around, he saw a beer bottle that had washed up on shore. He went over and picked it up and then came back and sat down.

"What are you going to do with that?"

He scooped up a handful of sand. "Ever hear of putting sand in a bottle so it won't float out to sea?"

"No."

"It's an old custom of mine."

"You're weird."

After filling the bottle, he held it at his side. "Let's walk a little more and then head over to the karaoke bar."

Emma walked along, carrying her shoes and commenting on how beautiful the stars were and how wonderful the warm sand felt sifting between her toes. "In a few months it'll be Christmas. Do you think we'll be seeing each other then?"

With a solemn expression on his face, he gazed into her eyes. "I sure hope so."

Emma, regretting the question she had just asked him, changed the subject slightly. "John, tell me about your Christmas last year. Were you home with your family?"

"No. I was in a truck with several officers from Battalion."

"Were you going to a Christmas party like they show on television, you know, with movie stars and pro sports players who flew into Afghanistan from the states to cheer up the troops?"

"I wish that were true. We were on our way to witness an execution."

She shuddered. "I don't want to hear about it."

"Three Afghan Army soldiers had been court-martialed for cowardice and sentenced to death by firing squad. These poor sons of bitches weren't cowards. The only cowards were their commanding officers. They managed to make scapegoats out of these guys after a botched patrol. What was ironic was that one of our officers tuned in Christmas songs on the truck's radio. As we got out of the truck, he left the music blaring. One of the condemned asked me to give his wife a letter. In the background, the song being played was *Have yourself A Merry Little Christmas* as the men were shot dead. It was then that I decided that, when my tour was up, I would never go to war again. By the way, I gave his wife the letter." He looked at Emma and saw tears in her eyes. "Sorry kid. I didn't mean to upset you."

"It's a wonder you didn't go insane."

"Well, I did drink a lot. Are you ready for some karaoke?"

Experience had taught John where the suspicious stranger would be waiting for them, probably an ambush to rob them or rape Emma. That would only happen over his dead body.

They climbed a wooden staircase back to the street. As they got to the last two steps, the stranger jumped from the bushes and confronted them with a hunting knife. "Give me your money or I'll cut you both."

John situated himself in front of Emma and sized up the thief. He was a skinny guy, unshaven and in his mid-forties. "Ever hear of getting a job, buddy?"

"Fuck you and your job. The money. Now." He jabbed the knife at him.

Emma cried, "John, give him your money."

John, cool and collected, realized that the thief had the high ground by one step. "Take it easy, mister. I'll get out my wallet."

"Hurry up, man."

With Emma hiding behind him, John pulled the wallet from his back pocket and held it out, but not at arm's length, to force the thief to bend down to grab it. When he did, John hit the thief's knife-hand with the sand-filled beer bottle, causing bones to break, and he dropped the knife, screaming in pain. In what seemed like a single motion, John let go of the bottle, caught the knife before it hit the step, and clasped it in his teeth.

The thief tried backing away but got tripped up on the top step.

John took that second to put his wallet back in his pocket. "Where do you think you're going?" He grabbed the scrabbling thief by his belt and dragged him headfirst down the stairs.

Emma screamed. "John, let's get out of here."

"I'm not done with him yet." With a look on his face that Emma had never seen before, John grabbed the thief's good arm and thrust the knife blade through his wrist, impaling him to the wooden step.

The thief screamed like a girl.

"A job would have been less painful, pal."

Emma was in a state of shock over the brutality she had just witnessed. "You stabbed him with his knife!"

"Hey, I only returned his property to him."

Emma stared at John in disbelief. She couldn't understand how he could be so flippant over the man's tortured condition. "He could die."

"Nah. He's not that lucky." After hailing a cab, John and a visibly shaken Emma got in and told the driver to take them to Paps Ultimate Bar and Grill.

The driver asked, "Which one?"

"By the O'Hare Hilton. Oh, and when you get a chance, call 911. There's a creep lying down at the bottom of those steps. I'm not sure if he's drunk or high, but I *am* sure he's in need of medical attention."

***

Walking into the karaoke bar, they heard a disc jockey say, "That was *Big Girls Don't Cry* by the Four Seasons. Let's hear it for Mike and Martha."

The crowd clapped and cheered.

After finding seats at a table, Emma signaled to the waiter. "I really need a drink. Bring me a Vodka Martini."

"Make mine a Seven and Seven."

"Right away, sir." He was off.

Emma slumped in her chair. "John, what if he had stabbed you with that huge knife?"

"Well, I guess I'd be hurting like hell...or maybe dead. But I'm not. He's the one hurting. Think of this as his lucky day, because if he had hurt you in any way, he would be dead right now."

Leaning over and kissing him, she whispered, "Well, thank you for protecting me. That was very scary."

"Emma, it's time for some plain talk. When we get back to Denver, I want to have an exclusive relationship with you. Tell me now if that's what you want also."

"It is. Actually, I'm glad you brought it up. If you hadn't, I would have asked you the same thing before we got back."

"I like the way you think, Emma."

Two hours, six Vodka Martini cocktails, and two Seven and Sevens (for John) later, a totally inebriated Emma stood up and, taking John by the hand, said, "Come on...we can sing better than these people."

"Emma, this is Oldies Night. I can't—"

"You can read the words, can't you?" Emma waved at the crowd and slurred out, "Somebody pick a song for us to sing."

The disc jockey said, "Tell us who you are and where you're from."

Before a not-so-drunk John could say a word, Emma announced, "I am Emma, Emma, hic, and this is my macho man...John...and we are both from...Colorado."

"So, John you're wearing the uniform of the United States Army Rangers. Am I correct?"

"Yes, sir. A captain, just back from Afghanistan."

"Let's hear it for John and Emma."

The crowd went wild as Emma downed the last of her cocktail.

The disc jockey said, "I have just the song for you two: *Will You Still Love Me Tomorrow* sung originally by The Shirelles. It was the number one song way, way back on February 12th 1961. Take it away Emma and John!"

John looked into Emma's bleary eyes. "All set, sugar?"

Each of them had a microphone and began to sing while stealing glances at each other.

As they sang the next line, Emma shook her hips and twirled around and then ran her hand down between her breasts while gazing lovingly into John's eyes.

Then a totally drunk Emma hugged John and rubbed his butt as they sang the next verse.

Emma covered up John's microphone with her hand and sang the last lines by herself while looking straight into his eyes.

As John and Emma got a standing ovation, the disc jockey announced, "Let's hear it one more time for John and Emma, and John, we all want to thank you for your service."

Emma went over and picked up some guy's drink, downed it in one gulp, and then announced to a very delighted John, "Let's go to bed in your room. I'm ready."

***

At 3:27am began the best twenty-two minutes of John's life. Emma came into his room wearing only her bra and panties. He was already stripped down to his boxer shorts. Seeing Emma standing there with a comely smile on her face, he pulled the covers off the bed without taking his eyes off her, and then rushed into her open arms. He started kissing her. As he did, she put her arms around his neck, and with her left hand on the back of his head, began to play with his hair.

John slipped his right hand up her side and pushed it up under her bra and felt the nipple on her left breast, causing her to sigh. He then continued to kiss her with great passion as he undid her bra and let it fall to the floor.

She stepped back and stared at him and slowly let her panties slip down to the floor. As she stepped out of them, she watched John remove his shorts. Now both totally naked, they stood there looking at each other for a minute before he picked up Emma and held her in his arms as if she weighed nothing. He carried her to the bed and gently laid her down. "I love you with all my heart." John lay down on his side next to her and began caressing her breasts. "I want you to be my lover and my wife. I never knew that I could be this happy. You are beautiful and sexy and smart." He then pressed his open mouth down on her left breast and softly licked her nipple.

Emma, getting more and more passionate and breathing very heavily, put her arms around him tightly and whispered, "I think it's time for you to do your duty, honey." She felt, with her hand, what she thought was the hardest muscle in his body and knew it would be for a while.

John reached over and threw off the one pillow that was still on the bed and proceeded to find love's last hiding place. It took about twenty minutes to consummate their love for one another, and Emma would not have minded if John made her see fireworks one more time. He lay there on that bed with no sheets or pillows on it with Emma in his arms. She though: I'm safe here in the arms of my lover and soon-to-be husband. The vodka martinis finally caught up with her, and she went to sleep contented in a way that she had never known in her twenty-nine years of life.

John lay there with his arm around her and her head rested on his shoulder. He looked at Emma and thought: I am the luckiest guy on earth. He didn't go to sleep right away. His mind returned to the battlefields of Iraq and Afghanistan. He recalled the faces of all those who were killed in action. It was then that he did something out of character. He thought: thank you, God, for being so kind to me.

***

They both woke up at 9:00am, but it was Emma who was in a state of shock. She shook John and yelled at him. "What are you doing in my room, and how did I get completely naked?"

Now John was wide awake. "You came into my room wearing only your bra and panties, which you promptly took off. What's the matter with you? Last night before we had sex we professed our love for each other. Maybe if you hadn't single handedly caused the bar to run out of vodka martini cocktails you might have remembered."

"I don't believe you."

After telling him not to look, Emma got out of bed and put her bra and panties on. John didn't look but did say, "It's a little late for that since I saw it all last night. I guess technically it was early this morning."

Emma did peek at John as he got out of bed and put on his boxer shorts. That didn't stop her from ranting about how he took advantage of her in a moment of weakness.

"Emma, what do you want from me? I love you and you said you love me. So we had sex. That's what two people who love each other do."

Emma yelled from her room. "I didn't expect it to be like this."

Now fully dressed, she stormed back into his room and added, "I was saving my virginity for my wedding night. Now there's nothing to save and it's all your fault."

"I didn't know you were a virgin, but I'm glad you are...I mean were. Once again, I love you and I want to marry you. What do you want?"

"I don't know at this very minute. I'm not so sure you didn't rape me. I could file charges against you. What do you think of that?"

"Since I took an oath to be an officer and a gentleman, you might get me sent to Leavenworth military prison for twenty years...especially in the age in which we live. I hope, if that's your desire, you'll wait until after I meet with my men. They'll be home at Fort Carson in two days. I wouldn't want them to see their CO being led off in handcuffs."

"I don't ever want to see you again, and if you ever need your glasses adjusted, go to Sears Optical. Don't come to see me, ever, you...you bad person!"

"Bad person? Hell, you thought I was pretty good last night."

Emma stomped out of the room and slammed the door to her side shut. John just stood there for a few minutes perplexed. He put on his ripe uniform and realized he couldn't comb his hair because he'd have to borrow Emma's comb, and that seemed out of the question now. He just put some water in his hair and ran his fingers through it. He went over to the door and knocked on it, hoping he could patch things up.

George S. Naas

No answer.

He knocked again and again but to no avail. He tried one more time and said, "Emma, please let's talk. I love you with all my heart." He pushed open the door and saw that the room was empty. His heart sank but he consoled himself by thinking that he'd see her on the plane.

***

He got to O'Hare and checked in and asked if Emma had checked in. After receiving a negative reply, he walked around the concourse, looking for her. Finally, it was time to board his flight to Denver.

He waited until they called out the last boarding announcement. Maybe he had missed seeing her in line, waiting to board. He hoped he would find her in her seat and that she wouldn't be mad at him anymore. But she wasn't on board. He took his seat and looked at the empty seat next to him. He thought she should be sitting there smiling at him. He remembered how her perfume smelled. In a plane full of people, he felt all alone. At the last minute, a large man struggled down the aisle and sat in Emma's empty seat.

The man said, "It looks like it'll be nice weather all the way to Denver."

John just looked out the window and said nothing. He thought: this trip is not going to end like this.

The man in Emma's seat tried to strike up a conversation with

John by thanking him for his service to the country.

John glared at him, perturbed. "If I had a dime for every time I heard that compliment... Hell, we have two and a half hours to sit next to each other, so let's make the best of it by ignoring each other, okay?"

"Hey, I'm sorry, man."

John went back to thinking about what Emma might be doing. She must've taken another flight. He thought: I hope she isn't going to start seeing that asshole Brad again. God, if he ever lays a hand on her again, I'll decapitate the prick with one punch.

***

Emma did book another flight to Denver but it hadn't left yet. She sat in a stall in the ladies restroom and looked at the selfie she'd taken of her and John in happier times at the Paps Ultimate Bar and Grill. She started to cry, thinking I do love him but does he love me or just want to get in my pants? "Well," she muttered. "He got what he wanted."

She really got distraught when the airport P.A. system, which had been playing random songs, just happened to play, *Will You Still Love Me Tomorrow?* She couldn't stand being alone in the airport, so she called her sister, Jane. With a melancholy tone in her voice she said as Jane answered, "I have to talk to you."

"Where are you? Are you in Denver? I thought your plane wasn't going to get here for three more hours since the Delta flight was cancelled."

"I'm still in Chicago and I'm terribly upset." She started crying into the phone.

"What's the matter...are you hurt...or sick?"

"No, I met a man and I spent the night with him."

"You did what?"

Little Maggie kept trying to take the phone away from Jane. "Let me talk to Aunt Emma, Mommy."

"In a minute, honey. Mommy has got to talk to Emma right now. How did all this happen so suddenly?"

"I'm sending you a selfie I took last night. We really fell in love. I think at least I did. No that's not correct. He loves me."

"I can't believe this. You're not some school girl out on prom night. You just took the term layover to an all new level."

"Please don't preach to me. I'm really hurting and I want your advice."

"I just got your picture. He sure is cute. What are all those empty martini glasses doing on the table?"

"His name is John Peterson and he's a Captain in the Army Rangers."

"You didn't answer my question. Who put away all of those martini cocktails?"

"I didn't notice that part of the picture."

"Well, look at it now."

A sheepish sounding Emma said, "John told me that I drank

too much, but I didn't believe him."

"Good lord, it's amazing that you didn't pass out."

"When I woke up I thought maybe he had raped me."

"Well, did he?"

"No. Now that I remember, I know it was consensual, but I didn't want to seem so easy."

"If he loves you, he won't think less of you for jumping in the sack with him on your first date."

"Damnit, Jane. He probably doesn't want to see me again."

"Does he live in Denver or Boulder?"

"Fort Carson. He's getting out of the Army in six weeks. I don't know what to do."

"Keep your chin up. He's not going to give up on you. When you see him again, be a little standoffish, as if he were a onetime thing."

"They just announced that my flight to Denver will begin loading in fifteen minutes. It's United flight 1411 and will be in Denver at 3:10 your time. Can you still pick me up?"

"Of course. I can't wait to hear more about the handsome Ranger Captain that got my sister to give something to him for free when other men would have given their souls for it. You two did use birth control, didn't you?"

Remembering that they didn't, Emma lied. "Of course."

***

On the flight back to Denver, Emma started counting backwards from last night. She thought: last night doesn't count. We had sex this morning. So this would be one more day. Then it dawned on her that one more day could have made things even worse from a reproductive standpoint. Now getting stressed out over it, she thought: all I can do is wait two weeks.

She went back to thinking about John and how sad he looked as she slammed the door in the hotel. I was a fool to do that.

***

Landing forty-five minutes ahead of Emma, John got on board a bus for the 95-minute trip to Fort Carson. All he did was think about Emma.

He thought about her so much that, when he got to Fort Carson, he didn't notice that he passed, shoulder-to-shoulder, the Commanding General of the Fourth Division without saluting.

The General said, "Just a minute, Captain. Were things so bad in Afghanistan that you forgot to salute a superior officer?"

John saluted. "My apologies, General, Seemans. It won't happen again."

***

Arriving twelve minutes late, Emma looked all over for Jane's red Toyota Rav 4. Jane pulled up, and as Emma got in, Jane hugged her. "Sorry I was running a little bit late. I stopped and got you a welcome-home present." She handed Emma a sack from Walgreens.

"What is it?"

"Take a look."

Emma reached into the sack and pulled out a small box. On the side of the box it read *Early Pregnancy Test*. She frowned. "Why did you get me this?"

"Because your tone of voice changed on the phone, so that made me think you were lying to me about birth control. Besides, you never could hold your liquor."

"Oh, Jane, what am I going to do?"

"Not panic, for one thing. Wait a few days and see what happens. You can't use the EPT that soon anyway, and by then he probably will have called you up, and you'll be happy again. Besides you might not be pregnant."

"What if I am?"

"We'll cross that bridge when we get to it. But something tells me you have found a really good man in a most unusual place, and I don't think he'll desert you. He's really good looking and you've already found out he's not gay."

Emma laughed and cried at the same time.

The commotion woke up a sleeping Maggie who was riding in the back seat. "Did you bring me something, Aunt Emma?"

"If she did, honey, it might be called a cousin."

"What's that, Mommy?"

"Well, honey—"

Emma shushed Jane. "I have a present for you in my bag. I'll give it to you when we get to my house."

***

Meanwhile, one hundred seven miles away in Fort Carson, John was at the officer's club, trying to console himself with a Coors beer while waiting for a call from base housing. He finished the beer just in time to receive the call confirming that his officer's quarters were set up. He could move in whenever he wanted. Walking to his quarters, he ran into an old Army buddy.

Captain Martin Richardson took one look at John and exclaimed, "John, you look terrible. We heard that Charlie 2-5 was coming home tomorrow. I thought that was still your company."

"Martin, do me a favor. All my gear will be arriving in a couple of days. You and I are the same size. Could I borrow some dress khakis from you?"

"Hey, anything for an old West Point buddy."

"You said 2-5 is arriving tomorrow? My boys got out quicker than I thought."

"John, let's go to my place. You can take a shower and get cleaned up, and Betty will be glad to see you. She's four months pregnant."

John thought: it must be catching, for all I know. Realizing what he just thought, he said to himself, "What if she's pregnant? She wouldn't give up on me then. If that were to be the case, she might still tell me to take a hike, though. Emma is a strong-willed woman."

***

Back in Boulder, Jane insisted that Emma come over for dinner the next night after work. Emma was glad to say yes. She felt that the only person she could confide in was Jane. Now back in her home, she didn't bother to unpack her suitcase. She sat down in her living room and stared at the Walgreen's sack. She finally got up the courage to take out the EPT box and leave it in the bathroom. Her thoughts returned to John and the wonderful times they had together.

Just then, the phone rang. The caller I.D. showed it was from Brad. She thought: if he keeps calling I'll let him meet John. That'll put the fear of God in him. Finally she went to bed and thought about how, just eighteen hours earlier, she was with her lover and how she may have ruined her chance to have found true love. Berating herself, she cried herself to sleep.

***

John sat in his quarters, thinking about Emma and picturing how she looked. He thought he'd give her a couple of days to get over being mad at him, and then he'll go to her office. He took out his wallet to look at her business card but could not find it.

He thought: I'll find her office if I have to see every optometrist in Boulder. In a fit of rage, he slammed his fist into the wall. If I

~45~

hadn't been so hot to get in her pants I might still have the woman I love. God, I'm an asshole. Hell, I better get some sleep. My guys will be here at ten-hundred hours. It'll be good to know that we are all safely out of that shit hole. I can't wait for my career to be over. I've paid for my West Point education in blood.

At nine-hundred hours the next morning, John walked into Hanger Three at the Fort Carson Air Field to wait for his men's plane to arrive. There were women and kids all over the place and TV news crews from every television station in Denver. At exactly ten-hundred hours, the military transport plane pulled up and the men of Charlie 2-5 disembarked into the waiting arms of their loved ones. Lieutenants Peoples and Gee and John were soon giving each other high-fives. Larry Peoples asked John, "In the text message you sent me from Chicago, you said you'd found the woman of your dreams. Were you kidding or drunk?"

"No, Larry, I wasn't kidding. I think that I might have blown it with her. I've never been so miserable in my life. I'll never forget the last thing she said to me. She called me a *bad person*."

"That's it? A bad person? Hell, every guy in 2-5 has called you a lot worse than that. For example, prick, asshole, cocksucker, and a stupid fuck."

"Yeh, but I don't love them."

"Man, since that's the worst thing she said, she'll forgive you and take you back. I guarantee it. Now if she had of said you're a dick who only wanted to fuck her, then that would be different."

"She wouldn't say that. She is a real lady."

"So you've got nothing to worry about. She...by the way, what's her name?"

"Emma."

"Emma, then, she'll find you."

"How?"

Larry waved for the TV news crews to come over.

"What are you doing, man?"

"Just watch."

The only crew to come over was from the local Fox station. Reporter Peggy Madonna stepped up and put her microphone in Larry's face. "How does it feel to be home?"

"It feels great. I want to introduce you to our Company Commander, Captain John Peterson."

"Hello, John. What do you think of your men?"

Having to shout over all the yelling and screaming and laughing, John said, "These guys are all great. I could never have served with a better bunch of guys. We always had each other's backs."

Larry grabbed the microphone. "Captain Peterson has a problem that your station can help him with."

An embarrassed John did his best to get Larry to cool it, but he wouldn't.

"Our Captain has a girl problem that we hope Fox News will help us with. His girl, Emma, is mad at him, and he is brokenhearted. We'd like you to send out a plea to Emma to give John a break and take him back."

Soon, all of Charlie 2-5 chanted, "Take our Captain back, Emma. Take him back, take him back."

"This is Peggy Madonna reporting from the very joyous homecoming for the men of Charlie Company 2-5."

John put his hands around Larry's neck like he was about to strangle him.

"John, you know you're glad I did that. Hell, man, you might get real lucky in the next twenty-four hours."

***

Fox News led off their five o'clock news with the *Where is Emma* human-interest story. Peggy Madonna said, "I don't know who this mysterious Emma is, but if you are watching this show, Emma, contact John right away. If you don't want him, I'll take him."

In Boulder, Jane was cooking dinner while her husband watched the news. She was not paying much attention until she heard Emma's name. Running into the living room she yelled, "Pause that!"

Her husband said, "What?"

"That's our Emma they're talking about. Pause it, pause it. Now run it back. Good! Now pause it and don't touch it."

Two minutes later, a downhearted Emma rang the doorbell.

A very excited Jane ran to the door. "Emma, your John is on TV right now."

"What do you mean?"

"See for yourself."

Emma stared at the TV in disbelief. "He really loves me and I really love him. Isn't he cute? And he's so strong and wonderful."

Jane said, "I know what you're thinking. You want to go be with your man. Be careful. Remember what you two did the other night."

"That doesn't matter now. Hopefully we'll do it again tonight." Now with tears in her eyes she added, "I love you, Jane, but I've got to go. I'll see you later."

"Don't drive too fast. Tell him he's a very lucky man."

"And I'm a very lucky woman. Bye."

All the way to Fort Carson, now a very happy Emma started making marriage plans. She thought: I don't need to think about the EPT. In fact, I hope it comes out positive.

Covering the one hundred seven miles to Fort Carson in record time, Emma pulled up and stopped at the main gate. Asking the Military Police how to get to the barracks of Charlie 2-5, the MP asked, "Are you Emma?"

As she answered his question in the affirmative, she thought: I wonder if John even knows that I'd seen the news show?

The MP was happy to give her directions, but after driving around and seeing how all the barracks looked the same, she stopped and asked two soldiers walking down the road if they knew the location of Charlie 2-5. Pointing at a house, one of them said, "You should go up to that really nice home on the hill. It belongs to

Commanding Major General Lyle Seemans. He'll be glad to help you."

"Thank you," Then she wondered why they walked away laughing.

Pulling up in front of the General's house, Emma thought: he has a really nice place.

She knocked on the door.

After a few moments, a plump short woman in her mid-fifties opened the door. "Can I help you?"

"I hate to bother you, but I'm looking for Captain John Peterson. I tried to find his barracks but I couldn't, so I asked two nice soldiers, and they suggested that I asked the General."

"Come on in. I'm sure my husband can help you." She turned around. "Lyle, this young lady is looking for one of your officers."

General Seemans marched into the room, and as soon as he saw her, he said, "You've got to be Emma."

She blushed. "Yes, that's me."

"So, you're the woman Captain Peterson has fallen madly in love with. Well, Emma, if he's still on the base, I'll have him brought over here immediately." Picking up the phone, he said in a commanding voice, "Check to see if Captain John Peterson is on the base." After about thirty seconds, he barked, "Good. Have him brought to my house right now." He hung up and looked at Emma. "He'll be here in a few minutes."

His wife spoke up. "Emma, dear, would you like a cup of tea

while we wait for your knight in shining armor?"

"Yes, Mrs. Seemans. That would be very nice."

"Please call me JoAnn." After serving Emma her tea, Mrs. Seemans said, "Now I want to know all about how you two met."

***

In the meantime, John got up off of his bed where he had been sulking and answered the knock on his door. To his surprise, two Military Policemen glared at him. "Are you Captain John Peterson?"

"Affirmative."

"We have orders to bring you to General Seemans' house."

"Now?"

"Right now."

John gulped. "What are the charges?"

"There are no charges, Captain, not that we know of."

The other MP added, "We were ordered to bring you to see General Seemans, and that's all we know."

John immediately got cleaned up and was shaking as he shaved. He was sure Emma had gone to the brass and accused him of rape.

Riding in the army jeep, he thought: shit! Emma is really out for my blood. I guess I'll be busted in rank and locked up in the stockade within an hour or so. I wonder what the hell she told the General, probably that she was too drunk to give her consent.

Jesus Christ! And Seemans could be one real hard-ass. By the book...God almighty. He'd believe her if she claimed I raped her.

Hell! With her beautiful sweet face plastered on TV, everyone in the whole damn country will be yelling, *Get a rope and hang his fucking ass.* This is bad, really fucking bad!

The MPs dropped him off in front of a huge house on a hill. With a clenched fist and a heart that was racing two hundred times a minute, he walked up to the front door and rang the bell, praying no one would answer. The General answered the door. John saluted him. "Captain John Peterson reporting to the General as ordered."

General Seemans returned the salute. "Come in, Captain."

He followed General Seemans down a long hallway, solemnly, as if he were being taken to the gallows, and all the time his heart was full of fear as he wondered what was coming next. He didn't have to wait long to find out.

He walked into the living room and practically fainted when he saw a smiling Emma sitting on the coach, holding a cup of tea.

"Hi, honey."

The General gave John the mandatory icy stare that all Generals do. "Emma was looking for you, Captain."

JoAnn said, "You have a lovely bride-to-be, John."

Speechless and in a state of shock, John managed to stutter, "Yes, yes, I am very fortunate, sir. I...I mean Mrs. Seemans."

Emma put down her cup, slinked up to him, hugged him, and then looked into his eyes. "I missed you, honey."

JoAnn asked, "Do you have a wedding date set?"

Emma hugged John. "Three weeks from this Saturday. Isn't

that right, honey?"

"Whatever you say, Emma."

"Where is the wedding going to take place? Do you have a church picked out?"

"I saw this pretty chapel while driving to your home, and I thought it would be a romantic spot for us to be joined together for the rest of our lives."

"Captain, we expect an invitation."

"Of course, General. Emma will be sending them out soon."

Emma, still tightly holding John's arm, said, "I want to see where you are living."

As they left, John snapped to attention and saluted the General. "Thank you, sir, and Mrs. Seemans, it was an honor to make your acquaintance."

JoAnn hugged Emma. "You two make such a nice couple."

Emma replied, "See you at the wedding."

As they walked down the path to Emma's car, General Seemans yelled, "Now I know why you missed our salute earlier today. You had something much more important on your mind."

"Thank you, sir."

Getting into Emma's car, a now somewhat sedated and relived John said, "I thought I was going to be shot."

"You *will* be shot if you try to back out of the wedding. You just found out that I have friends in high places."

"I would never back out. I love you with all of my heart."

"John, I'll never be mean to you like I was the other morning. I'm so sorry that I acted like such a fool. You *do* forgive me, don't you, John?"

"Of course I forgive you."

"John, honey, I'm going to make it up to you. Your place has a bed, doesn't it?"

"Yes, but I haven't tried it out yet."

"Then, sweetie, we'll just have to break it in together."

***

Thirty seconds after closing the front door to his quarters, John was ready to get down to the business of lovemaking. Emma, on the other hand, explored his quarters. She investigated the kitchen and the bedroom while John was relieving himself of the two beers he had drunk before the Military Police knocked on his door.

Rushing out of the bathroom, he looked all around and found Emma on the balcony that overlooked the airfield. She was leaning on the banister and watching long lines of troops board an Air Force transport.

John came up behind her and put his arms around her waist and kissed her neck.

"I wonder where they are going."

In a very solemn tone, John answered, "Where I just came from. We are Charlie 2-5. Those boys are Alpha, Baker, Charlie, Delta, and Echo companies in the third Battalion, 3-5. Their families are crying tonight."

"I'm sorry for them, John, and I will pray for their safe return." She crossed her chest. "But I'm thankful you're here with me and you'll never have to go back."

"If they can capture or kill Mohammed Bin Alsharadi, known as the White Fox, then things can change for the better. He runs the whole show in Afghanistan for the Taliban."

"Won't they just get someone else to be their leader?"

"That would be pretty hard for them to do. The only other insurgent who raised hell with us was his son, Rafiq Bin Alsharadi. He won't be bothering our boys in 3-5. You remember when you were fixing my glasses and asked me about the mark on my frames?"

"Yes."

"His son was the one who put it there."

"You said you killed him."

"Yeah, I did. His old man took it pretty hard and put a one hundred thousand dollar reward out for killing me. He said he would double it if I were captured alive."

"Thank God I didn't know you then or I would've worried myself to death."

"It's pretty damn hard to capture an Army Ranger alive. We usually keep one grenade to use on ourselves as a last resort. That way, at least, we can take a couple of those sons of bitches with us."

"John, let's go to bed now and not talk about it anymore."

"Okay." He couldn't hide the delight in his voice.

"Here's how things are going to work." She led him to the bedroom. "In here, you will outrank me, but in everything else we are equal."

"Well, then, since we *are* in the bedroom, I want you to take off your clothes while I lay propped up on the bed and watch the show."

"You bad boy." Emma removed her white high heels then her rose colored skirt, followed by her white blouse. Next her bra came off.

John never took his eyes from her voluptuous form. "Your breasts are absolutely beautiful. Keep going. Remember, this is your Captain speaking."

After slowly and sensuously removing her panties, she stood there naked before him. "Now it's your turn."

Changing places, John removed his clothes, not slowly, not sensually, but more like they were on fire. Emma didn't take her eyes off John either.

He jumped on the bed, and as he did, the bed frame broke, dumping them both on the cold tile floor. They got up laughing, pulled the mattress off the broken frame, and put the sheets and blanket back on it.

Emma sniffed the blanket. "Why does this smell like mothballs?"

"We get them out of supply where moths are always a problem. If not for the mothballs, we'd be sleeping under a blanket full of holes."

"They should make them out of something other than wool."

"The Army likes wool."

Sticking her tongue out at him, she commented, "I don't like it. It's scratchy. I'll buy a new one tomorrow."

"Then it won't be regulation."

"I don't care. End of discussion. Now kiss me, Captain Regulations."

As they lay there on the mattress on the floor, John caressed her breasts and lavished her neck with butterfly kisses.

"John," she said, hoping he wouldn't stop kissing her. "We didn't use a condom the first time, when you took my virginity, and I don't take birth control pills since I wasn't having sex with anyone."

His moist lips moved down her throat to the soft valley between her breasts. "Uh, huh," he muttered and kept moving downward. "So?"

"I could get pregnant..." She gasped as his tongue explored her bellybutton. "In fact, I might be pregnant already."

"So," he breathed and continued licking downward.

"But soon, I'll be Mrs. John Peterson, so it really doesn't matter if I'm pregnant now, does it, darling?"

At the upper reaches of her soft and curlies, he stopped kissing her and looked up. "I'd be the happiest man on earth."

"Good." She pushed his head back down. "Now make me the happiest woman on earth."

He proceeded to kiss her, this time taking the ultimate dive into heaven.

Her entire body shuddered with delight. "Keep doing that." She gasped. "Don't stop. It's getting me really turned on." She thought: he does this so well...*gasp*...he must have a lot of experience with women. For whatever reason...*moan*...they didn't latch their claws into him, I don't care. He's mine now.

She reached down and touched him, pleased that what he was doing to her made him ready for action. "Now, John. Do me now."

He gently got on top of her and propped his weight on his elbows so he wouldn't crush her small frame. "Is that an order, ma'am?"

"Captain, do your duty."

As they consummated their love for each other, she heard the roar of the plane's engines and said a silent prayer for the departing soldiers. As the roar dissipated into the night sky, she thought: I'm so glad he's not going with them...*gasp*...that we'll be together forever.

John was all man. All muscle, but a gentle lover, teasing her ear with his lips as his breathing rose to a fever pitch. She matched him push for push, and as his body stiffened and a moan escaped his throat, she too found that final step over the edge of bliss.

They lay there in silence, still joined, hugging each other and catching their breath.

Emma had been thinking, though. She'd never been loved like this before, and the thought of her being pregnant because of this love made her future with John seem like heaven on earth. "Just think," she whispered. "You could be a father next year."

"I'd love to have a little John Jr. or Emma girl in the family. Of course, it may take a while. We may have to do this a lot more often."

She patted his bare fanny. "That's true, but any one of the millions of sperm you just put inside me might have already made our baby a reality."

"There can't be a million of them."

"I think I know quite a bit more about how the human body works than you. If however, dear, I ever need a machinegun fixed, I'll let you handle it."

John pulled out, sat up, took hold of Emma's left hand, and plying her for sympathy, said, "I'm sorry that I must seem stupid as hell."

"That's what happens when you have a one-track mind."

"Hey, I'm a red-blooded American male. What did you expect?"

"A loving husband. I'll take care of the rest." Feeling that she had just won a minor victory, she smiled. "Now give me one of your Army Ranger kisses."

As he did, he slipped his hand down between her thighs.

"We just did that. You can't be ready to do it again."

"I think my sperm boys need some reinforcements. It's the Ranger Way."

A giggling Emma looked in John's face. "Like jumping out of a plane?"

He rolled over on top of her. "That easy."

She felt him enter her again, this time with more force and determination to pull that ripcord again. "The Ranger Way, huh?"

"Consider this a tandem jump."

She did, and the fireworks were better than ever.

After falling asleep in her lover's arms, Emma woke up about 2:00am and put on John's shirt. She inhaled his scent and felt an arousal she hadn't expected. Just the smell of him turned her on.

It dawned on her that she had lost track of what day it was. She got her I-phone out of her purse and discovered it was now Saturday. Two more days with John before she had to go back to work, how fast would the hours tick away?

He woke up and felt around in the dark for Emma and then saw her on the balcony, looking out at the now deserted airfield. She was wearing his shirt. "Now what is she worried about?" he mumbled and got up off the mattress. Walking up behind her, he slipped his arms around her midsection. "My shirt's a little too big for you, honey. But if you're right about being pregnant, you'll grow into it quickly."

"John..?"

He felt her body tremble in his arms. "What's bothering you, Emma?"

"There's no way the Army will send you back, right?"

"To Afghanistan?"

"To war, John. Any war."

"No way." He kissed the back of her neck. "I'm all yours,

baby."

She turned in his embrace to gaze into his eyes. "Promise?"

"You're being silly." He picked her up. "It's time for the Ranger Way."

Putting her head on his shoulder, she chided him, "Do you ever think of anything else?"

"Once in a while." He laid her back down on the mattress. "But I'll let you rest up so we can do it again at seven-hundred hours. I can't think of a better way to start the day."

Waking up a little later than he had planned, he got up and looked around for Emma. Her clothes were gone...and her purse. "What the hell?"

The front door creaked open. She pushed her way in with a McDonald's parfait for herself and a big breakfast and an orange juice for John and coffees for both. "You don't have any food in this place."

"I've only been here for less than twenty hours."

She arranged the meal on the small dinette. "I slaved over this. Sit down and eat."

As they ate their breakfasts, Emma checked her voice mails and emails. "Dammit."

"What's wrong?"

"Brad keeps pestering me. He wants us to get back together. There was never any together. John, I'm kind of afraid of him. What if he bothers me and you're not there to protect me?"

"I'll pay him a visit and he won't ever bother you again."

"Maybe I should let the police handle this."

"What can they do?" He sipped orange juice. "Nothing. I'll get results."

"You promise you won't hurt him like you did that guy in Chicago?"

"You know I can't promise that."

"I don't want you to wind up in the stockade."

"All right. I won't hurt him."

She sipped her coffee. "Can you get leave to go with me to Boulder?"

"I have thirty days right now, and then two weeks left in the Army. I can go wherever I like. However, I want to be back down here this Sunday for a cookout that First Lieutenant Larry Peoples is putting on for us. 2nd Lieutenant Nathan Gee will be there along with Sergeant Major Tennyson Henry. Their wives and a couple of kids that Nathan has will be there too. I think you'll like them and I know they'll love you. Sergeant Major Henry is the old man in the outfit. He has more hash marks down his sleeve than you can count."

"What's a hash mark?"

"It's a service stripe worn on the left sleeve to indicate three years of service in the Army. One stripe for every three years. I always tell my boys, that when the rounds start coming in, to get as close to Sergeant Major Henry as they can get. He'll keep them alive."

"What would you be doing?"

"Getting as close to Henry as I can, too. Remember, I'm only stupid on pregnant stuff. I'm pretty smart on staying alive. Three combat tours is proof of that."

"John, we'd better get in that morning Ranger Way you talked about last night so we can get on the road to Boulder."

Grabbing Emma and folding her over his shoulder, he carried her to the mattress and, after plopping her down, he began to tickle her feet.

Emma kept laughing, and while trying to get his hands off her feet, she accidentally kicked him in his chest. It had no effect on him.

"I won't stop until you tell me who you love."

Giggling Emma said, "You, silly, with all my heart."

After making love, John and Emma took a shower together and dried each other off with well-laundered, army-issue towels. John took his towel and rubbed it all over her hair. He then kissed her and slowly wiped her breasts and, taking hold of both of her shoulders, pulled her toward him. He kissed her supple mouth, her chin, her neck, and on his knees now, he kissed her navel and carefully caressed her thighs as he patted the water off. He then stood up and put the towel around her shoulders and hugged her and wiped the droplets off her back.

Now it was Emma's turn to dry off John. She held up his left arm with her right hand and then slowly moved the towel up and down his arm, gliding over muscles that felt like steel, first the one arm and then the other. She then turned to his chest, wiping away the water that had collected on his pecs and in the deep crevices of his six-pack abs. Bending down and wiping his thighs, she saw that he was ready to make love again. She hung the towel on his erection, stood up, and kissed his cheek. "We have to get going...can't hang around here having sex all day."

They finally got their clothes on and headed for Boulder with John driving Emma's car.

"John, does anyone in your family know who I am?"

"No, I haven't contacted my family yet. I will when we get to Boulder. How about you?"

"My sister Jane and her husband know. But no one else."

"That's not exactly true. We were all over Fox News. Everybody knows our names. Hell, the show might even get you some new patients from all over Denver. I know I'm going to give you all my business."

"Not if you're planning to pay me off with Ranger Ways."

"Hey, that's not a bad idea."

Getting to Boulder, Emma wanted to stop by her office. She gave him directions until: "Here we are...1345 30th Street, the red brick building. See my sign?" *For Your Eyes Only Optical.*"

Looking around Emma's office, John said, "I'm impressed." He went around picking up and trying on different frames and asking Emma how he looked.

She just stood there with her arms folded, thinking how he could act like a kid one minute and be her lover and a soldier the next.

He tried on a pair designed for a woman. "How do I look?"

"Childish."

He took them off and motioned to a hallway. "Let me see the rest of your place."

Walking down the hall, Emma pointed to a room. "This is one of my exam rooms."

"Well, maybe you should give me an eye exam. I've noticed that if I drink several beers and a couple Boiler Makers, the next morning my vision is kinda blurry. Is that anything serious, Doctor Emma?"

"It's called a hangover. Sit."

"Your exam chair is very comfortable."

"You know what? I'll give you an exam. It can't hurt. Besides, what if I see something? Leave your glasses on. Take the paddle and cover your right eye and read the smallest line you can."

"Okay, LEFODPCT"

"Now switch over and cover your left eye."

"LEPODRCT"

"Close, but you're reading 20-20. Now take off your glasses. I am going to put some drops in your eyes to check your pressure. Look at the blue light and open your eyes really wide. First we'll check your right eye. Now we'll check your left eye. Oh, my God!"

Now a concerned John said, "What's the matter?"

"You have a big problem."

"What is it?"

"But I can fix it. Close your eyes and keep them closed." She then kissed his left eye and then the right and then his lips. "You're all better now. That'll cost you a hundred dollars. It would have been cheaper but I charge extra for kisses."

A wave of relief washed over him. "You had me freaking out there for a minute. Isn't it unethical to scare the hell out of a patient?"

"I suppose it's also unethical for me to kiss a patient, but I *did* enjoy it."

Trying to pull Emma over to sit on his lap and realizing that the chair was only made for one, John declared, "I guess I won't turn you into the medical ethics board this time."

"John, I have some catching up to do since I've been gone a month. You still don't have any civilian clothes with you. Why don't you go get a new suit? I want you to look really great when you meet my sister and her husband and daughter for dinner tonight."

"I'll get something that looks good but no suit. Something casual, but first I have something to take care of right away."

"What is it?"

"I just have to call Fort Carson about something. It's no big deal."

Leaving Emma to her work, John made a cell phone call while leaning on her car. "Is this the office of Doctor B. G. Daynes?"

"Yes. Who's calling?"

"My name is Jerry Grimes. I realize that this is asking a lot, but I wondered if there is any way I could see the doctor today. I've been told he deals with soldiers suffering from PTSD and I'd really appreciate it if you have an opening."

"As a matter of fact, we've had a cancellation. It'll cost you three hundred and fifty dollars, paid up front, in cash. We don't accept military insurance—"

"That's not a problem. Thank you, I'll be over in ten minutes."

Walking into Doctor Daynes' office, John was met by his secretary, June. "I'm Jerry Grimes. I called a few minutes ago."

"Of course. Give me the $350.00 payment in cash, and then you can see the doctor."

John paid June and she pushed a buzzer that opened the door to an inner office. Doctor Daynes didn't get up from his chair behind the desk. "Have a seat."

He sat in a rickety wooden chair, indicating the doctor was a cheap bastard.

"Jerry is it?"

"Yes."

"I want you to know that I have never been fond of the military, and you're mistaken that I treat PTSD. However since you're here, what can I do for you?"

Before John could say anything, the doctor's intercom came on. "Yes, June?"

"I'll leave the $350.00 in the desk drawer, and I have to ask you about Monday's schedule."

As they talked, rudely interrupting the appointment, John sat there sizing up the doctor. He was about thirty-five with a burly build, maybe five-foot-ten, and he couldn't weigh over two hundred forty pounds. He had a small goatee, beefy hands with hairy knuckles, but a squeaky voice that didn't fit is stature.

"Good work, June. You can go home now." He turned back to John. "So, Jerry, what exactly is your problem?"

"It's about a girl. She thinks I'm stalking her. She also claims that I've sent her threatening emails and I'm trying to force her into having a sexual relationship."

"Before you go on, I want you to know that this behavior is something that I'll have to report to the police."

"Actually, my name is not Jerry. My name is Captain John Peterson, and I'm here to tell you, Brad, that you're going to have to report *yourself* to the police, you worthless piece of shit."

"Here, here, now—"

John stood and leaned over the desk. "If you value your pathetic life, you're going to leave Emma Mansfield alone."

The doctor reached for the phone. "I'm calling the police. You can't come in here and threaten me."

John slammed his hand on top of the phone, trapping the doctor's hand. "I can and I just did." He pushed down on Brad's hand so hard that he winced.

"Stop! You're hurting me."

"Emma has proof that you've been stalking her and sending her nasty emails and leaving her rude phone messages. So go ahead and call the cops now, Brad." John released Brad's hand.

He retracted his hand and massaged it. "The police won't be necessary. Tell her I won't bother her again. It was just a misunderstanding."

"Was it a misunderstanding when you grabbed her arm and twisted it so hard you left a bruise the size of Texas?"

"I didn't mean to."

"I have an idea, Brad. How about I put my hands around your neck and squeeze it until your eyes pop out of that ugly head of yours? I can always say I didn't mean to."

"Please...don't hurt me," Brad whimpered. "I swear on my mother's grave that I'll never call or bother Emma again."

John huffed. "Brad, I know you'll never bother Emma again. In fact, I'm sure that if you see her on the street, you'll walk to the other side...no, you'll run to the other side and look the other way. If you decide to get brave when I'm back at my base, think again. I've killed many men in battle. It wouldn't faze me a bit to add you to that list. Shit, I could always say I didn't mean to rip off your head and piss down your neck." John patted Brad's cheek. "Capisce?"

Brad folded his arms on his desk. "I understand."

"I'm really glad we had this little talk. Now give me back my goddamn $350.00 and I'll forget this every happened...unless you get stupid and call her again."

"I won't. If she presses charges, I could lose my right to

practice medicine in Colorado."

"Get my money."

Brad scrambled out of his chair and rushed to the outer office, his hands covering the wet spot in the front of his pants.

John got out his cell phone and called Emma. "I'm here in Brad's office. He won't be bothering you ever again."

"You didn't kill him?"

"Nah, just made him wish he'd died of embarrassment."

"John, did you hurt him?"

"I think he pissed on himself, that's about all. See you in just a little while, honey."

Brad came back with John's dough. "Tell her I'm sorry."

"You know, Brad, you should work out. Maybe join a CrossFit club. You may be a big guy but you really are a pussy." John pointed to Brad's crotch. "And you should change your diapers."

***

Emma was waiting for John outside her building. When she saw him drive up, a big smile came across her face. He thought how pretty and sweet she looked, holding her purse with both hands on the straps. She rushed to the car. "I was shocked by your phone call from Brad's office. Tell me what happened."

"He may drag his knuckles when he walks, but the guy is a first-class wimp. He thinks he's a tough guy around women, but he's a pussy around an Army Ranger. When I told him who I was and why

I was there, he pissed in his pants."

"I would love to have seen the expression on his face."

"Well, you won't see his face anymore. He told me to tell you he's sorry. I wouldn't be surprised if he moves out of Boulder. The thing I enjoyed the most was patting his cheek and telling him *Capisce.*"

"What does that mean?"

"I guess you haven't seen *The God Father*. I saw it five times in Afghanistan. The bottom line is that he understands the severity of his misunderstandings."

"You're my hero. Now what can I do to repay my hero and lover? I know. After we leave my sister's and go to my place, I'll let you have your way with me."

"The Ranger Way?"

"And I have nice blankets on my bed and not that nasty army wool. Just don't jump on the bed. We don't want to break two in one day."

Pulling up in front of Jane and Larry Miller's house, Emma uttered, "Darn it! That black Buick in the driveway, it's my mom and dad's car."

"You weren't expecting them?"

"Be nice, John, and get ready to be raked over the coals by my mom. The first thing she'll want to know is if you're a Catholic."

"Never mind that I'd survived three tours at war."

Emma opened the front door and looked at John. "Here goes."

Just as soon as they walked in, Emma's parents met them. "Emma." They hugged.

"John, this is my dad, Robert, and my mom, Carol."

John shook Robert's hand and Carol gave him a hug. "I've been looking forward to meeting the two of you."

Carol spoke up, "So, John, do you go to church?"

"Whenever I can. There aren't many opportunities on the battlefield."

"What denomination would you be?"

He shot a quick glance to Emma, one that meant *thanks for the warning.* "It varies from week to week."

Carol didn't back down. "John, is there one you prefer over the others?"

"I don't think much of church. Brick and mortar. Tile and glass. Not much good to a soldier when bullets are flying all around."

"Emma is a very staunch Catholic, and I know she wants to find a man who shares her faith."

"When I see an American soldier in a body bag, I don't care what his faith was."

Just then Jane walked in, with a little girl in tow, and held out her hand. "I'm Jane, Emma's sister, and this is my daughter, Maggie."

John accepted her handshake then pulled her in for a quick hug.

Maggie, standing with one foot kind of turned toward the other and one hand clutching a stuffed toy dog (and looking as cute as can be) said in a shy tone, "Are you and Aunt Emma getting married?"

"Maybe, Maggie, if she'll have me."

Bending down to eye level with Maggie, Emma said, "Yes, honey, and John will be your uncle."

Jane intervened. "After seeing you on the news, John, I feel like I know you already. I hope you like fried chicken and mashed potatoes."

"I love it."

"My husband, his name is Larry, he has to work late so you'll meet him later."

"I'm looking forward to it."

"The food is all on the table so everybody take a seat."

Maggie sat next to Emma then John, Robert, Carol, and then Jane.

Carol spoke up. "Emma, dear, would you say the blessing?"

Emma, already perturbed with her mother, bowed her head, and she was glad to see John do the same. "Thank you, dear Father, for us getting together for this meal. Thank you for this wonderful man and the love of my life who is sitting next to me and who will be my husband three weeks from today."

Carol gasped. "What?"

"Amen," Emma finished.

"You can't be serious."

"You heard what I said, Mother."

"I have a say in this matter. He's not Catholic."

"No you don't. And I don't care."

"I didn't raise you to forsake the church."

"God doesn't care either, and I don't give a damn if we're married by a justice of the peace."

"Sad, sad, sad." Carol kept shaking her head.

John sat stoic, more afraid of Carol than the Taliban.

"I do have some happy news for you, Mother. There's a pretty good chance that early next year you'll all get to come to the christening of our baby."

"The church will never allow it."

"We'll do it in a river if we have to."

Robert laughed. "John, you're getting a real firebrand for a wife. Congratulations. I think this is great news. Don't worry about Carol. She'll come around."

Holding Emma's hand tightly under the table, John replied, "Thank you, sir."

A sheepish Carol said, "At least ask Father William Pierce to marry you."

"I'm way ahead of you, Mother. I contacted him this afternoon and he agreed to conduct the ceremony. He doesn't care that John's not Catholic. He only cares that I'm happy. Our wedding is going to take place in a chapel at Fort Carson."

Jane gave Emma a big smile, and then gave John one too.

Unknown to everyone, events put in motion 7,600 miles away would have a direct bearing on the fates of Emma and John. But that worry was three weeks away. Tonight, after saying their goodbyes and giving more hugs, John and Emma drove to her house and went to bed. After again enjoying the Ranger Way, they lay there content in each other's arms and fell fast asleep.

***

After sleeping in late and enjoying coffee and donuts and orange juice at a newly opened Dunkin Donuts shop, they drove back to Fort Carson for the cookout, stopping only to buy some beer. It was their contribution to the party.

Getting back in the car with the beer, he whispered in Emma's ear, "Sorry, kid, they were all out of Vodka Martinis."

Emma elbowed him in the ribs.

"Oh, God, that hurts. I think my ribs are broken and I might have a punctured lung."

"Well, you asked for it."

"You might have to kiss it and make it better."

"Later."

Arriving at the home of First Lieutenant Larry Peoples, they were greeted by Larry's wife, Ann. "Come on in. So you are Emma, the one who stole John's heart. The boys are in the backyard."

Taking Emma by the hand, Ann led her to the kitchen where she met Lynn, the wife of Lieutenant Nathan Gee, and Mary Jo, the wife of Sergeant Major Tennyson Henry, and Betty, the wife of Captain Martin Richardson. Emma, with a big smile on her face, hugged all the ladies. She noticed that seven-year-old Timmy, the son of Betty and Martin, kept rubbing his left eye.

"Mommy, my eye hurts."

Emma examined Timmy's eye. "Betty, your son probably has bacterial conjunctivitis. In other words, pink eye. You'll have to keep him away from the other kids since it's contagious. Is there a pharmacy on the base that would be open on a Sunday?"

Ann said, "Yes. It's right by the infirmary."

"I'll drive," Betty said.

Emma and Betty walked up to the counter where Emma showed the pharmacist her credentials and told him what she needed. "Make it eye drops, not an ointment. Kids hate ointments."

"It's against regulations for me to fill a prescription that's not from a base doctor. Good luck getting an appointment on Sunday."

Just then General Seemans' wife, JoAnn, walked in and perused the antacid aisle.

Emma rushed to her and explained the situation. "He won't accept my prescription."

JoAnn stormed over to the pharmacist, Sergeant First Class Langely. "Fill her prescription now."

"I'm sorry, Mrs. Seemans, that would be against regulations."

"The child needs this medicine. Fill the prescription now, Sergeant First Class Langely or the next time I come in here I'll be addressing you as Private Langely."

The rattled Sergeant said, "All right, Mrs. Seemans. I'm sorry I upset all of you. Just trying to do my job."

Emma added, "I also want some artificial tears, the ones that come in the single-use capsules."

After thanking Mrs. Seemans and telling her the time and place of the wedding, Emma and Betty went back to the party.

"Let me get this straight." John sounded perplexed. "You walked into the base pharmacy and got a prescription filled? I think that's against regulations."

Emma had an answer for him that he couldn't argue with. "John, we're married to men in the Army. We're not enlisted in the Army, so we don't care about your regulations. Capisce?"

With a grin on his face, he just stared at Emma. "Yeah, sounds logical to me." He bit into a burger fresh off the grill.

"Your hamburger looks like it wasn't cooked enough."

"It tastes perfect."

"Oh well, it's your body."

"Hey, I'm washing it down with a beer. That'll kill all the germs."

"Wow, John, you could be on to something there. You should submit an article to JAMA. They might say you have come up with a new way to treat diseases of the large intestine."

"What is JAMA?"

The Journal of the American Medical Association.

He took another bite of his almost-raw burger. "How much does it pay?"

"You're incorrigible."

Once the eating and most of the drinking was over, the women and men congregated in their own groups. The men reminisced over their experiences in Iraq and Afghanistan. Then they took off their shirts and got into a water balloon fight. It was every man for himself. Soon there was water dripping off bulging biceps, super-pecs, and glistening six-pack abs. Emma watched in amazement, thinking: just weeks ago, John and his friends were in desperate battles to survive, and now they're running around half naked and playing children's games as if nothing had ever happened.

The women just watched and moved back out of range, not wanting to get wet. Then they went back to talking...about the men mostly.

Emma threw a question out to the other women. "John likes to use the term *Ranger Way*. Is that something he dreamed up or is that a real Ranger saying?"

Ann, Lynn, Mary Jo and Betty all burst out laughing.

Mary Jo, the oldest of the group, said, "Honey, I have heard that line weekly for the last twenty years. Yes, it's a Ranger thing, and there's something similar in all in the other branches of the military. They just change the name, Navy way, Marine way, etc. We all know what it really means, don't we, girls?"

Betty said, "Once you two are married he'll slowly get over it. Right now you're new to him. Remember you can always say, 'No Ranger Way tonight.' It's a good way to make him suffer for something he did that you didn't like."

"That would be mean."

Ann said, "I agree with Betty. The Army likes to say they mold men into the best soldiers on earth, which they do. Well, Emma, it's the job of us five wives to mold our five soldiers into the best husbands on earth. Unfortunately, for the five of us, it seems like that's going to take a lifetime."

Ann left to get a pitcher of iced tea and check on the kids.

On the men's side, Martin announced that he wouldn't be enlisting for another three years. He said his enlistment would be up just one month after John's, and his fellow officers and Sergeant Major Henry would become civilians.

John said, "So, Martin, how are things at Army Intelligence? Has the White Fox raised the reward on me, dead or alive?"

"Not that I'm aware of, but if he does and you keep pushing your boys now that you're all back, one of them may turn you in for the reward."

"Hell, they're all on thirty days of I and I (Intoxication and Intercourse). They should all love me."

Grabbing Tennyson Henry by the arm and shaking him he said, "This is the guy they should all be pissed off at. I'm a sweetheart. Tenny is the hard-ass."

"Okay, Martin, since you're going to cash in your chips like us, why not join our new business venture?"

"We're going to provide security for everything from Marijuana growers to providing safe passage for ships going past Somalia in the

Gulf of Aden. We can get $200,000 per trip."

"John, what kind of muscle would we have on board the ships?"

"Not as much as you would think but enough. Right now all the pirates have to do is fire a couple of AK rounds at a ship and the captain gives up. But when three ex-Rangers with AR-15s and a forth with a fifty caliber open up on them, the pirates won't know what hit them. We're also thinking about adding a couple of M-9 Antitank Rocket Launchers. There's no law saying we can't fire them at those crappy boats the pirates have."

"John, I'll think it over." He then went around and gave everyone a high-five. "Guys, it's been fun. Thanks again, Larry."

The women were ready to call it a night, too.

Emma told Betty, "Put the drops in Timmy's eye three times a day and use the artificial tears—that will help when his eye itches. He'll be fine in a couple days. Remember to wash your hands a lot."

While driving back to Boulder, Emma looked at John. "What's the plan for tomorrow?"

"I've got some paperwork to send to Battalion, so if I can use your car, I'll be back by the time you close your office."

"What are our plans for tonight?"

"I hope the same thing as last night." He reached over and put his hand on her thigh.

"Watch the road. At the rate you want to have sex, our wedding night will be just another rerun."

"No, it won't. Being with you, every time seems like the first."

"Honey, you really know how to be sweet, even when you lie."

"Emma, there *is* something that you *could* do for me. One of my men, Corporal Charles Leatherwood, has been to see eye doctors at Walter Reed Army Hospital, and he's still can't hardly see with his right eye. They're telling him it's battle fatigue because they can't find anything wrong."

"John, could it be battle fatigue?"

"I doubt it. They sent him to see a military psychiatrist because they think he's trying to get out of the Rangers. I know this kid. He did two tours with me. He sure as hell isn't a chicken. I'm afraid some of the army shrinks are inclined to go with what the brass wants to hear. It could ruin his career."

"I'll take a look at him, but I don't know how I'll find something they missed. They have the best and most expensive optical equipment in the world, and military doctors are among the finest in the world."

"The one thing they don't have, though, is you. I fear he's just another number to them. He lives in Broomfield, and he is on a thirty-day leave. I could have him in Boulder tomorrow, if you have an opening."

"How about four-thirty? Everyone will be gone by then. I'll get his history and check him over to the best of my ability."

"Good. I'll call him in the morning."

After arriving at Emma's home, John took off his shirt so she could rub his back while he sat on the edge of the bed. She reached around and felt of his dog tags then pulled the chain they hung on up and over his head so she could see them better.

John Peterson: O17595313

Blood Type: O negative

Religion: Methodist

"Why do you have two of them, in case you lose one?"

"Because one stays with my body and the other goes to Regimental...if I get killed in action, that is."

"Don't ever say that to me again, not ever, you hear! You'll never see action again. You promised me."

"And I keep my promises, Emma."

"I hope you do promises better than you do the truth." She left the bedroom.

"I never lie to you." He turned on the TV and started flipping channels. "Jezze." When he came upon the local Fox channel, he couldn't believe his eyes. He hit the *pause* button. "Emma, come here. Get a load of what's on the news."

She returned to the bedside and looked at the screen. "My god. My mother? And who is that woman with her?"

John sighed. "It's my mom."

"How nice. Now I know what your mother looks like. Take it off pause and let's find out what they're talking about."

"This is Peggy Madonna reporting, and I'm here with the

mothers of Captain John Peterson and our mysterious Emma. Fox News broke this story a few days ago when Charlie Company returned home from Afghanistan. When we interviewed Captain Peterson, he was really depressed. It seemed, at that time, he had broken up with his girlfriend and wanted her back. No one knew who the mystery woman was, just her name. Emma. Well, tonight we're going to find out." She turned the microphone to Emma's mother. "Carol, tell us who she is."

"She's my daughter, Emma Mansfield. She's a Doctor of Optometry and has her own practice in Boulder. If you need an eye exam and glasses, you'll find her at *For Your Eyes Only Optical.*"

"So, Mary, you are John's mother, and you have some great news for our Fox viewers. Tell us what it is." She pointed the microphone at Mary.

"John and Emma have not only patched up their little quarrel, they're getting married in three weeks. My husband, Edward, and I haven't met Emma yet, but she has to be a wonderful girl for our John to have fallen in love."

"So, Carol, do you know where the wedding will be held?"

"At Fort Carson in a chapel. Our priest, William Pierce, will marry them. Peggy, here is a picture of Emma."

The camera zoomed in.

"She is very pretty. All of us here at Fox News wish John and Emma the very best." Looking directly at the camera, Peggy said softly, "We'll be right back."

John grabbed Emma and pulled her up close. "So what do you think, sugar? Are you proud of our moms?"

"Thank God my mother didn't bring up the Catholic thing again."

For once they just lay together, naked but no Ranger Way. Emma was grateful just being in the arms of her lover. Kissing John on his neck, she said, "Goodnight, honey."

They fell asleep.

About 3:00am she awoke from a dead sleep. John was mumbling, some sort of Military jargon she couldn't understand. "niner-niner-zero...niner-niner-o." Sweat soaked his hair, which he whipped back and forth in a frenzy. "Get down. Get down."

"John." She shook his shoulder. "John, wake up."

He gasped and sat straight up in bed, glanced around, his eyes wide with terror. "What...where am I?"

"It's all right. The war is over for you."

Recognition and relief lifted the dark cloud from his face. "Fuck." He lay back down and wiped sweat from his forehead with the back of his hand. "Sorry. My biggest fear is going back to the sand...another eight months of hell all over again."

She pulled the blanket off him. "You're not going back. It's okay. I'm here with you."

They slept the rest of the night under a sheet.

The next morning as she lay beside him, she thought to question him about his nightmare, but then decided not to bring it up. He'd tell her if he wanted to. While making coffee, she wondered if he was keeping from her the really bad things he'd lived through over there.

John got up at six, and after leaving Corporal Leatherwood's phone number with her, he kissed her goodbye and drove back to Fort Carson.

Having two patients cancel their appointments gave her the opportunity to see Corporal Leatherwood at 11:00am that morning. She called him and set it up.

He was very prompt. When he walked into Emma's office, she saw he was very young, only twenty-two, she guessed, but built like all Rangers, solid muscle, but at six-foot-four inches tall, he stood three inches taller than his Captain. He had blue eyes and dirty blond hair, and his smile was extremely shy. She shook his hand. "Come with me, Corporal, to my exam room."

"Yes, ma'am."

"Have a seat. Make yourself comfortable. I'll be right back."

Sitting in the exam chair, he glanced around at all the eye charts and machines then immediately stood up when Emma came back into the room with a clipboard.

"Relax, Corporal."

"Call me Charles, okay?" He sat back down and stared at her. "I saw your picture on Fox News. You're even more beautiful in person."

"Thanks." She wrote something on the clipboard. "I'm sure my fiancé would agree."

"Captain Peterson is the greatest captain that Charlie 2-5 has ever had."

"I'm sure he'd disagree." Emma stepped up to the chair. "Before I examine your eyes, tell me when your problem started and which eye is affected."

"First, doctor, I want you to know that I'm not trying to use this problem to get out of the Rangers."

"You're not? You sure?"

"I love the Rangers."

"Okay, now that that's settled..."

"Oh. It is my left eye and I started having problems in Kabul."

"Sand, sun, anything extreme get in your eye?"

"Ah, no, nothing."

"How about bugs? They do have bugs in Afghanistan, right? I know they have snakes."

"Bugs, ah, no...wait a minute. I forgot...I got bit by a Sandfly in the corner of this eye. Yeah, I totally spaced it when I was at Walter Reed... I mean, it only itched for about a week, almost drove me crazy, but it finally went away, so I thought no more about it. But now that you mention it, I noticed a little bit of my side vision in that eye wasn't the same as it had been."

"Did it ever hurt or feel like something was in your eye, sand, gravel, smoke?"

"That's exactly what if feels like now, but more so."

"What do you mean, more so?"

"It feels like there is something inside my eyeball."

"Hmmmm." She inspected his cornea with a bright light, pulled back the lids and found nothing foreign. "No sign of irritation...I can't get your records from Walter Reed so I want you to tell me what their doctors said."

"One said I have a lot of floaters in the eye but that was not uncommon. They'd go away eventually because of my age. Another doctor wanted me to see a shrink because he said, I was just a pussy. I'm sorry. I mean a coward."

"Charles, I'm going to dilate both your eyes so that I can compare them. Did any of the doctors at Walter Reed mention to you about parasites indigenous to eastern Afghanistan?"

"No. They mainly just kept saying for me to do my duty and quit trying to get out of the Army."

"Now lean your head back and open your eyes as wide as you can." She put in the dilation drops. "There. It'll take about a minute for them to dilate. Did you receive any blows to the back of your head recently?"

"I had a mild concussion when a round exploded a few feet from my bunker, but that was last year. The thing I remember about that, as I tried to get up, two Taliban insurgents came running over to finish me off, but Captain Peterson shot one dead and then killed the other one in a knife fight. Well, he only wounded the guy, but seein' as how Captain Peterson wasn't taking any prisoners, he knifed him again, right in the throat. I watched it all while leaning against the front tire on the Humvee Peterson drove up in. I was dizzy. My ears were ringing, but I know what I saw. Captain Peterson saved my life. He's a hero."

"You were lucky he was around."

"One of the damndest things I ever saw was when the Captain was helping our interpreter question a Taliban leader. All of a sudden, the sandrat spit in the Captain's face. He just calmly wiped off the spittle, took out his forty-five Colt, and shot the bastard right between the eyes. Man, we fretted over that for days. The General was going to bring him up on charges, court-martial our Captain for murder, but Peterson didn't take crap from anyone. Turned out the bastard was HIV positive, so the General deemed the shooting self-defense. Then there was the time Captain Peterson got into a fist fight with a Marine grunt—"

"I don't need to hear about that, Charles. Thank you very much. Now let me look into your eye to see what's going on."

Emma examined both eyes. "You do have a lot of floaters in that eye, but I'm not so sure they're normal floaters. The pressure is also different in each of your eyes."

"Is that bad?"

"Charles, just close your eyes and relax. I'll be right back."

Emma called a colleague, Doctor Rich Lindahl. "Richard, I have a patient in my office right now. He's a soldier."

"Your fiancé?"

"What? No he is not my fiancé. He is, however, in my fiancé's company. The reason I'm calling is because I believe he has a classic case of visceral Leishmaniasis. The kid is going blind in his left eye. No one at Walter Reed picked this up because he forgot to tell them about a Sandfly bite he'd suffered. I would like you to verify my findings, and if you concur, where can we get the orphan drug, Paromomycin? It has fewer nasty side effects. Rich, you know as well as I do, other drugs will work but may practically kill our patient in the process."

"Emma, you're certainly correct. It *will* kill the protozoan parasites, of course, so will a nuclear bomb. You're also right about getting Paromomycin. Problem is, if the large pharmaceutical drug companies can't make money on a drug, they just won't make much of it. I guess they don't call those drugs "orphans" for nothing. I'll check around to see if I can get hold of enough of the stuff to help your young patient. Have him come over to see me at nine tomorrow morning."

"Pro bono?"

"Sure, anything for our servicemen."

"Thanks, Rich. I owe you one."

Going back to see her patient, Emma looked at him seriously. "I think what you have in your eye is a parasite. A friend of mine will see you tomorrow morning to confirm, and then we'll get you fixed up as good as new."

"Thank you, Doctor Mansfield. What do I owe you?"

"It's on the house and so is your appointment tomorrow. It was nice meeting you, Charles. I'm going to tell John that he's lucky to have you in his company. I'm sure he'll agree."

***

Meanwhile, John was sitting in on the latest intel coming out on the Nangarhar province from Army Intelligence, and the developments weren't good.

Driving back to Boulder, he kept thinking it was in Nangarhar province where the Fifth Ranger Battalion had lost twelve Rangers in action, thanks mainly to the White Fox. Seems shit had hit the fan there again.

Picking Emma up at her office, the first thing he said was, "What did you find out about Corporal Leatherwood?"

"I'm pretty sure he has a parasite in his eye but it can be cured."

"Goddamned Walter Reed. They should have caught that."

"In all fairness, the Corporal forgot about one insect bite, didn't tell them, so they had no reason to look for a parasite. If he hadn't come to me, your young soldier could have died if the parasite worked its way into his brain. Most of the time, it'll just get into the patient's intestines."

Driving to her home, he put his hand on her shoulder. "Emma, you are absolutely amazing."

"I'm not that amazing. I did go to school and learn everything I could about the eye. I'm still learning." She sighed. "John, my practice isn't going to interfere with our relationship once we're married, will it? You'll have your security business and I'll have my patients."

"Of course it won't affect our marriage...unless you don't give me a discount on my next pair of glasses."

"I think you can count on that."

Sitting at the dinner table eating a spaghetti and meatball dinner they had picked up at the Blue Parrot Restaurant in Louisville, Emma played with her food. "John, Corporal Leatherwood told me some things that happened in Afghanistan that I'm sure he made up."

John took a slug of wine. "What did he say?"

"You killed a man for spitting on you. I was sure Charles was joking, but then I thought, why would he joke about something like that?"

"Is that all?"

"Well, no. You killed a man in a knife fight, a man you could have let live and taken prisoner."

"Now, is that all?"

"Well he kind of mentioned that you got in a fight with a Marine."

"So, Emma what's your point?"

"It all sounds so barbaric and not something the man sitting across from me would do to another human being, not the man I love."

"But I did do those things." He poured himself another glass of wine. "Although the Marine won the fist fight. He was tougher than I thought."

"But those men you killed—"

"Screw those guys! When they say war is hell, it's not just a play on words, Emma. It's the real McCoy. Capisce?"

Looking down at her food, she said, "Well, I'm glad you'll never have to go back."

"There's a saying that everyone who's served in Afghanistan knows to be true: You can take the soldier out of Afghanistan but you can't take Afghanistan out of the soldier."

"What exactly does that mean, John?"

"I'm a different man now than who I was when I signed up...after those bastards knocked down our buildings with our own airplanes. What you see is what you get. I'm loyal to a fault, and I'll love you forever. Don't dwell on my past. It'll drive you crazy."

"I suppose you're right. At least you'll have some great war stories to tell our grandkids."

"Whoa there, Nellie. One step at a time, please."

"John, it's a really nice night. Let's go sit in my front porch swing and finish our wine together."

With his left arm around her and her head tucked into his chest, he swung the swing as they talked about their upcoming wedding, though Emma did most of the talking on that subject. She kept reaching out with her foot to touch the front porch railing but couldn't reach it.

"What are you doing?"

"Trying to touch the railing like you can do."

"You're not tall enough. You need to grow some more."

"I'm beginning to think that the only part of me that's going to be growing pretty soon will be my belly, and that'll be because of you, sweetie."

Putting his right hand on her stomach and softly patting it, he said, "Maybe you should not have drunk so much in Chicago."

"I still think that you took advantage of my inebriated condition."

"Do you really believe that, or do you want to believe it so you don't have to feel guilty?"

"Would you have taken advantage of me?"

"Hell yes! I thought about having sex with you the first moment I saw you. But I didn't get you drunk. You did that all by yourself. You kept downing those Martinis and moving that cute butt around while you sang, well, I have to admit you became a target of opportunity."

"A target of opportunity?"

"That's military jargon. If a target of opportunity presents itself, you go after it, especially if there's only a slim chance you'd achieve your primary target."

Running her hand through his hair, she questioned, "So I wasn't your primary target? It was probably that cute little flight attendant on the plane."

"Let me start over. If a primary target, because of circumstances, becomes a target of opportunity, then Army regulations say it's my duty to go after it."

"In other words, John, what you're trying to say is that it's the Army's fault if I get pregnant, and I could have General Seemans put in jail because you were just following regulations."

"No, no! I'm not saying that at all."

"Must be the wine jumbling up your thoughts."

"I shouldn't have brought up the target of opportunity because it only applies to enemy combatants and not to beautiful and sexy women."

"I'm glad to hear that, otherwise you might have shot me."

Getting flustered, John put his face right up to Emma's, and jamming both feet down, he stopped the swing. "If you could go back to that moment when you were standing in front of me wearing only your bra and panties, would you change events so you and I never happened?"

"You know I wouldn't. I love you. You don't see me complaining about the Ranger Way, do you?"

At that moment the chain holding the swing on John's side pulled loose from the porch ceiling, causing the swing to come crashing down at an angle. Emma screeched as she slid into him, and they ended on the porch in a tangle, but he didn't spill a drop of his wine.

"I guess this is the end of swinging for tonight."

"What do we do now?"

"Well, let me think, Emma. Hmmm. I can't think of anything."

"I know, John. I'm going to make you my target of opportunity."

"That's one great idea." He picked her up and carried her to the bedroom, kissing her all the way. After their lovemaking episode, they again went to sleep in each other's arms.

At seven the next morning, as Emma was taking a shower and getting ready to go to work, John's cell phone rang. He answered it.

"John, this is Martin. When can you get back to the base?"

"What's up?"

"I have something that I need to talk to you about."

"I can be there by eleven-hundred."

"Meet me outside the small PX by the parade ground."

"See you then, Martin."

John hurried as fast as he could to get on the road after dropping Emma off at her office. All the way to Fort Carson, he wracked his brain, trying to figure out why Martin was being so secretive. He knew by the tone of his voice that it had something to do with Army Intelligence.

Emma was busy getting ready to see Father Pierce at his church two blocks down the street at 11:00am. She was looking forward to the visit. The same could not be said for John seeing Martin.

Getting to the (PX) Post Exchange five minutes early, John saw Martin waiting for him in the parking lot.

"What's with all the hush hush?"

"John, when you guys came back, three of your men decided to take one week R & R in Istanbul."

"Yeah. Tenny approved their request, knowing you would have approved it if they had asked you."

"Who are they?"

"PFC Brent Ogden, Corporal Thomas Pepper, and PFC Steven McElwee. What did they do, get in a fight in some bar and get locked up?"

"I wish that was the case, John. They were supposed to report in at Regimental yesterday, six-hundred hours. No one has heard from them. To make matters worse, a mole that we have in White Fox's headquarters says three Rangers have been kidnapped and are being taken somewhere in the Tangi valley. Intelligence indicates that the White Fox plans on making an example out of them during Ramadan."

John's stomach sank. "Tell me they're not our Rangers."

"Our guys will be wearing orange jump suits with assholes standing behind them, blades at the ready to cut off their heads for the cameras."

"We can't let that happen."

"We have an entire Battalion moving that direction. They'll find them and bring them home."

"Martin, that's not good enough. Not for my men. I still have close to a month left in service before I muster out and become a civilian. I think that I can get one platoon of volunteers out of Charlie Company to go with me to get them. Do you think you can sell the idea to Division HQ?"

"Maybe, but how are you going to sell the idea to Emma?"

"I'll tell her we have to train some new recruits for the incoming CO who's taking over when I leave and transfer the flag to him."

"John, you'll still need an interpreter. I'll go with you, but what about the wedding?"

"I'm going to tell Emma we have to get married a week from this coming Friday. I think she'll go for it. She's not the big wedding type, though she'd probably love the end of the ceremony when we walk under a saber arch of crossed swords. It's impressive to see and to be part of."

"If she doesn't grab one and run you through with it for lying to her."

"God I hope she understands."

***

In Boulder, unaware of what transpired one hundred miles to the south, Emma was at The Sacred Heart of Jesus Catholic Church, meeting with Father Pierce.

"Emma, I am so happy for you. I have watched you grow up into the wonderful and beautiful woman that you are now. John must be quite a guy to have captured your heart."

"He's truly the best man I've ever known. He's kind, smart, good looking, funny, and I feel safe when I'm with him. I'm not saying that he's perfect...far from it. When he protected me in Chicago, I saw a side of him that I didn't like. He became vicious. And I've heard some very unsettling stories about him in the war. He's been a warrior for a thousand days, his life always on the line for our country. He's killed men in battle, Father, but sometimes I think he has no remorse for what he has done, and yet I'm proud he survived the hell, and I love him so dearly."

Father Pierce took hold of Emma's hands, and staring into her eyes, spoke in a soft manner. "Emma, you can't read his mind so you don't know if he regrets doing what he had to do in the heat of battle. I believe he probably *is* sorry for some things he's done. Our Savior said we should turn our swords into plowshares, but I don't think he wanted us to lie down and be slaughtered. There are forces in this world that are pure evil. Only a few men have risen up to stop them. Your John is one of them. You *should* be proud of him, and I think he deserves you."

"I'm proud of his service, Father, but now it's someone else's turn to protect or country. John's time as a soldier is almost over, and I want us to spend the rest of our lives together in peace."

Her cell phone rang. She looked at the display. "Please excuse me, Father, this is my sweetie calling." She answered. "John, you'll never guess who I'm talking to right now."

"Your priest."

Emma groaned. "That was just a lucky guess."

"Emma, ask Father Pierce if we can move the wedding up to Tuesday or Wednesday rather than that Saturday. It's only a few days earlier."

"I've already told my friends. They're expecting the wedding to be on Saturday."

"I don't think we can get the chapel for Saturday."

"Yes, we can. I've already booked it. John, Father Pierce wondered if he could meet you tonight. We don't have anything planned. Let's take him out to dinner."

"Okay. I'd like to meet him."

John heard her say, "Father, could we meet at seven tonight at *Three Margaritas* on 28th street. John likes Mexican food."

"Emma, tell John I'm looking forward to meeting him tonight."

"I heard," John said. "Talk to you later."

Hanging up the phone, she said to Father Pierce, "You'll really like him."

A beaming Emma spent the next two and a half hours discussing with the Father about marriage and getting a baby christened in the Catholic Church.

"You're not even married yet, Emma."

"No, the christening isn't for me, of course not, but for a friend."

"Oh, I see." Father Pierce looked at Emma suspiciously.

Just then they heard footsteps in the hall that made an echo in the near-empty church. They heard John asking someone where he could find the Father.

Emma ran out of the office and hugged John. "I want you to meet Father Pierce."

John, putting on a forced smile, said, "Sure, I would love to." Whispering in Emma's ear, he added, "I thought we were meeting him for dinner?"

"We are, but you can at least say hello since you're here."

Taking John by the hand, she led him into Father Pierce's office. "Father Pierce, this is the love of my life, John."

As John stuck out his hand to shake the hand of a smiling Father Pierce, he instantly sized him up as trustworthy and sincere. "I'm very glad to make your acquaintance, sir."

"And I'm glad to make yours, John."

"So, Father Pierce, I guess we'll be seeing you in just an hour or so for dinner."

"I think that's Emma's plan."

"Then Emma and I must be going so that I can get cleaned up."

Emma said, "See you then, Father."

Getting into the car, Emma looked puzzled. "John, are you just shy of clergymen, or is something bothering you?"

"Sorry, honey. I had a tough day." He had no idea how to tell her what he'll be doing four days after they get married.

"Well, I'm glad it had nothing to do with Father Pierce. I've known him since I was seven."

Father Pierce got to the *The Three Margaritas* a few minutes before John and Emma walked in. He was watching one of the large screen TVs. It was on CNN news, the reporter telling the world about the missing Rangers. John and Emma came over and sat down.

The Father said, "This is really bad news out of Afghanistan."

John cleared his throat. "Yeah, I know about it."

Emma elbowed him. "Well, I don't. What happened?"

The Father spoke up before John could say anything. "The Taliban captured three Rangers from Charlie Company 2-5."

Emma looked at Father Pierce and then at John, "That can't be right, John, That's your company. All your men got home safe. Right?"

"We thought they did, but three of my men were not on the transport plane."

Emma's adrenaline burn rose in her veins. "What happens next?"

"We're formulating a plan to get them back."

"I hope that plan doesn't include you."

"It probably won't."

"John, what exactly does probably won't mean?"

"We have an entire Battalion of boots on the ground right now. They don't need me. They're more than capable of getting my men back and killing the White Fox and every one of those murderous sons of bitches that makes up his joke of an army."

"John, we're in the presence of my priest. Please watch your language."

"Sorry, Father."

"That's quite all right, son."

They ordered their food, and as they ate their dinner, a somewhat more calm Emma told Father Pierce how she and John had met and how it was love at first sight and how she can't wait to become Mrs. John Peterson.

***

Back at Emma's house, they sat in the porch swing that John had fixed.

Emma cuddled up to him and pressed him about his missing men. "Did you know them?"

"Of course. I know all the men in my company. We really are a band of brothers. We would lay down our lives for each other. We've bled for each other, laughed together and cried together and froze and suffered in the heat together, and we went without food and water together."

"Well, for sure the Army won't send you back. Isn't that right?"

"I'd have to volunteer, but I'm not needed," he lied.

"Thank God, thank God, that's a relief."

Changing the subject, John told her Martin had decided to join the new business venture when his tour was up.

Emma, rubbing John's hand and then putting his hand on her belly, said while looking out into the darkness, "I really think that I might be pregnant. My body's cycles have always been very punctual. I'll know in a few days when I take the EPT test. You really wouldn't mind, would you?"

"Of course I wouldn't mind. I'd be happy if you were pregnant, and if our kid needs glasses, I can take him or her to Sears Optical like you told me to do in Chicago."

"I was upset in Chicago, but that was because I didn't realize how much I'd come to love you. Our child probably won't need glasses anyway. Things have moved so fast for us, John. The spat that we had seems like an eternity ago."

"Spat! You tried to beat me to death and then you wanted to have me shot. The only way it could have been worse is if you could have had me drawn and quartered."

"Well, you did steal my virginity."

"Do you want it back?"

"No, and besides, losing my virginity is a onetime thing."

"Good. I was kind of worried there for a minute."

"I know, let's replay how I lost it in the first place."

"The Ranger Way?"

"No. Maybe we can think of something new and exciting. Race you to the bedroom."

***

The next morning, Emma went to her office only to be met by an irate patient demanding that she should do something about the floaters in her right eye.

John arrived at the orderly room of Charlie 2-5 where his office was like all offices for Commanding Officers of Army companies. It had a spartan appearance. He had a plain wooden desk and two chairs that had seen better days going all the way back to the '60s. He had his nameplate on his desk, and in a corner leaned the company flag with a "C" in its center and the numbers 2-5. On the wall hung plaques of their unit citations and a few pictures of men who had paid the ultimate price for Charlie Company and the United States Army. He also had his sidearm lying on the desk.

Into this setting at ten-hundred hours walked Beverly Ogden, the mother of PFC Brent Ogden, one of the missing soldiers. Master Sergeant Phillip Lilja knocked on his door.

"You may enter."

"Captain, there's a lady here to see you."

"Send her in."

Walking into his office and standing in front of his desk, a plump and short woman with gray hair stared him down. "I'm here to find out what you are doing to save my son and bring him home."

"Please sit down, Mrs. Ogden. Would you like a glass of water?"

"No thank you."

John put the sidearm in the desk drawer and picked up the phone. "Hold all my calls."

Walking out from behind his desk and leaning on the edge, he looked at her grief-stricken face. "We're doing everything we can to bring him home to you. He's a good soldier and an outstanding Ranger. The Army will always protect its own. Right now there are plans being put in motion to rescue Brent, Thomas, and Steven. I can't tell you any more than that except to say I will be personally involved in the rescue. I hope you'll keep this information to yourself. You wouldn't want to do anything that would jeopardize our rescue mission and the life of your son."

John sat there talking to her for an hour and looking at the pictures she brought of Brent when he was growing up. The last one she wanted to show him was Brent wearing his dress uniform with the Ranger patch on his left shoulder.

Her hand was shaking as she handed John the picture. "He's so proud to be an Airborne Ranger. Please bring him home, Captain Peterson." Then she began to cry.

John gave her a hug. "Everything is going to be okay."

As she left the orderly room, the phone rang. It was Emma. "You would not believe how stressful a morning can be."

"Yes I can, Emma. What's going on with yours?"

"Some people are never satisfied. When do you think you'll be back?"

"Sixteen-thirty hours."

"What?"

"Four-thirty."

"See you then, honey. I'll have hugs and kisses for you."

Just then Sergeant Tennyson came in. "Sir, I'm getting emails from everyone in C Company, and to a man, they're ready to go back and get our guys, and that includes me."

"I already had your name penciled in, Tenny. I want you to put a list together. I think the best snipers we have are Cpl. David Bridges, Cpl. William Chesley, and Pfc. Paul Stanton. Tenny, tell them they're going to have to drop three Taliban fuckers from about two hundred yards while in deep grass. They won't have a chance for a second shot so they better not miss."

"I'll tell them to get their asses over to the rifle range at six-hundred hours tomorrow for training fire, sir."

"Tenny, tell everyone you pick that this mission is twofold. The primary target is to get our boys back. The secondary objective is to kill all the insurgents. These assholes are the baddest of the bad. We're not taking any prisoners. I mean none. I don't care if they are sixteen or sixty and every age in between. Shoot 'em all."

"Affirmative, Captain. I'll make sure that everyone gets the message."

Heading back to Boulder, John kept thinking about what to tell Emma. Running late, he got to her office just as she was closing. He got out of the car and opened the passenger door for her. As she got in, the blue skirt that she wore got pulled up on the seat, exposing her leg halfway up her thigh.

She saw John looking at her leg, so she raised up in the seat just enough to pull her skirt back down. "Don't even think about it. I'm starving. That can be your dessert for later."

"Emma, I have no idea of what you are talking about."

"You know exactly what I'm talking about. The bulge in your pants is giving you away. You must think about sex twenty-four hours a day."

"I didn't until I met you, sweetie. But with a girl like you who has the most beautiful breasts in the world, what else can I think about? Did you know your nipple on the left is just slightly pointed down and the right one is pointed up just a tiny little bit?"

"When we get home I'm going to look in the mirror to see if that's true."

"Emma, look at me. I love you, so I don't mind this slight blemish."

"Blemish! Listen buster, you're very cute and your six-pack muscles are gorgeous, I'll give you that, but your sagging pecs are giving you girlie boobs."

With a look of astonishment, "No."

With a smile on Emma's face, "Yes."

"Well, how about from the navel down? See anything you like?"

"I guess it's okay."

Now getting a little annoyed, John said, "What's okay?"

"Your leg muscles."

"Anything else?"

"I can't think of anything."

"You can't think of anything? How about what's between my legs?"

"I don't give it much thought."

"I guess you wouldn't. You're too busy saying, *Don't stop now, honey. Oh, oh that feels so wonderful.*"

"That's true. It does feel wonderful for forty-five seconds."

John smiled. "Truce?"

"Yeah, honey. Truce."

Sitting down at a booth in Red Lobster, John couldn't tune out the news about the missing Rangers being held by the Taliban in the Tangi valley. He watched with disgust as a Senator from Texas was saying how we need to go get our Rangers.

"What's this *we* crap? He ain't going anywhere. Charlie 2-5 is..." As soon as he said it he realized the blunder he'd made.

Emma took the fork out of her salad and held it in her hand like a bowie knife. "What do you mean your company is going back? You said the Army couldn't send you back unless you volunteered."

John stared at her open-mouthed.

"You did, didn't you? You volunteered."

"We'll only be gone for a little while. I'll be in the rear and not on the line, directing the rescue. I'm still getting out of the Army on schedule."

She dropped her fork. "I don't believe you, John. Those are your men. You won't be in the rear. You'll be on the line where the danger is, so don't lie to me."

"I'm not lying."

"Take me home. I've suddenly lost my appetite."

On the drive home, Emma burst out crying. "You don't have to go. You said the other battalion was going to rescue your Rangers. Do I have to become a widow before I'm even a bride?"

John pulled the car into a small park and shut off the engine. "I have to go, and so do my men. We know the terrain and the people who live there. I've received dozens of emails from the family members of my missing Rangers. They're all begging me to save them. Every Ranger in C 2-5 has volunteered to go back for this one last mission. I don't want to go. I thought I was soon to be done with the military. But I have to go."

"If you really love me then you won't go."

"What kind of life can we have if I don't do my best to save them? I would live every day for the rest of my life with the faces of those Rangers etched in my mind. For God's sake, Emma, you said if I really love you I wouldn't go. If you really love me you would know why I have to go."

"You've made up your mind and I've made up my mind, too. I'm calling Father Pierce right now and he is going to marry us this Saturday, in his church, and when you get back, and you damn well better get back, we'll have a real wedding with the crossed swords."

She dialed and listened, then: "Damn it, he doesn't answer!" Reaching into her purse, she took out a blue strip. "Do you know what this is?"

"No. What is it?"

While laughing and crying at the same time she said, "This is the

EPT evidence that you are going to be a father. Our baby is not going to be born without a last name. Our baby will bear the name Peterson and so will its mother."

Reaching over and hugging and kissing her, John whispered "I *will* come back to you, and no baby will ever have as good a mother as you will be."

"I just want the father to be around. So you have to return home safe. Capisce?"

"Yeah, capisce."

After a sleepless night of tossing and turning, Emma got up and called Father Pierce.

"Emma, what's wrong? Why are you calling me at 3:30 in the morning?"

"Because John's company has to go back to Afghanistan next Tuesday. We want to be married in the church this Saturday."

Father Pierce sat up in his bed and turned on the lamp next to him. "I thought he couldn't be sent back unless he volunteered."

"He did volunteer. His whole company did. All I can do is pray every day and night that God will protect him."

"Don't you want to wait on getting married? What if—"

"No." Emma ran outside and sat in the swing. "We want to get married so that our baby will have a real father if John doesn't come home alive."

"What? You're pregnant?"

"Father, don't preach to me on your morality. I won't be

coming to confession asking for forgiveness because I had sex with the man I love. I don't give a damn what anyone thinks. Will you marry us on Saturday or not?"

"Of course I will."

"Thank you, Father, and goodnight."

He put his phone down, got on his knees, clasped his hands, and prayed for John and Emma.

***

In the sweltering heat of the Tanji valley, three Rangers sat blindfolded with their arms tied behind their backs, trying to give each other encouragement that things would okay.

Corporal Pepper whispered, "Captain Peterson and 2-5 will come for us. I know it."

"I hope he hurries up. We're gonna run out of days," Private first class Mc Elwee said.

Private first class Ogden said solemnly, "Well, one way or another, we won't be eating urine soaked bread anymore. If we don't make it out, I hope my mother never knows how I died."

***

In Boulder, John and Emma got ready to go get their marriage license. Emma was not mad at John anymore. She understood and accepted what he had to do.

John broke the silence as they drove to the courthouse. "Last night was the first night that we didn't have sex."

"We'll be missing it a lot until you come home. That should be a big incentive for you to come back in one piece."

"I'm sorry. I never imagined anything like this could happen. I don't know why the hell my Rangers would go to Istanbul and walk around wearing their Ranger uniforms. If they had just come home with the company, things would be so different right now."

They parked outside the courthouse, and as they walked past a *30-minutes-only* parking sign, John, in a fit of frustration, slammed his fist into the sign, making it sway back and forth. Rubbing his sore knuckles, he said, "I *am* coming back to you. Remember this day two weeks from now. We'll be together and all our worries will be a thing of the past."

She kissed his hand. "Come on, honey."

Walking up to the county clerk's office, John was the first to notice the sign: *Closed until Monday.* "Jesus Christ! Okay, we drive to Denver."

A compassionate Emma hugged him. "Things will be all right."

After getting their license in Denver, they arranged with Father Pierce to marry them at 2:00pm on Saturday. Then they made a hurried trip to Hurdle's Jewelry. After buying a matched set of rings for Emma and a wedding band for John, they left them to be resized then drove to see both sets of parents and each of their sisters. These were the only people invited to the wedding.

***

Back at Fort Carson, Martin was going over the latest intel from the Tanji valley. The intel showed that the Taliban had moved up the Rangers' execution date to Thursday the following week. They were to be beheaded at sunrise. The intel from Forward Operations Base Miller showed that there was a lot of activity going on around a small village close to the Pakistan border. Martin thought: odds are that's where our Rangers are being held, one of the most dangerous places on earth. With this information it was time to call John.

"What's up, Martin?"

"John, we'll be saying our goodbyes at one-hundred hours on Wednesday. We've been given the green light. We had to move the schedule up. The White Fox doesn't want to wait much longer to kill our Rangers."

"Martin, I'm getting married tomorrow. As it is, Emma and I will have to wait until we get back for a real wedding and honeymoon."

"John, remember that shithole of a town, Abbas Koshteh? We have pretty good intel that our guys are being held there. Now for the bad news."

"I don't need to hear it. We'll be dropped in at night. That's the only reasonable thing to do. It'll be pitch black because of the moonless sky. They won't see us coming. We'll be landing in the grassy fields about two miles south of the town."

"It sounds to me like you have it planned out pretty well, John."

"They don't call us Airborne Rangers for nothing. My boys are used to the idea of a night jump."

"This is going to be pretty hairy, John."

"Martin, Tenny is getting everything in order. I want to spend what's left of today and this weekend with Emma. I just hope it won't be the last hours we have together. See you about fifteen-hundred hours on Monday."

Emma had been out of earshot, busy talking to John's sister, Ellen, and had no idea what had transpired. "John, I really like your parents and your sister. Ellen is so sweet. We're going to get together when you get back. Ellen and Jane are going to help me plan our real wedding while you're gone."

John did his best to give Emma a really upbeat answer. "That's really great. Why don't we go for a walk? Let's go to that park over there."

"This will be fun. I walked around Wonderland Lake Trailhead several times. It's a little over a mile. I hope you can handle it, being a big strong Ranger and all."

John put his arms around Emma's waist, and as she rubbed his biceps he kissed her and thought how utterly horrible it would be for her if he were dead one week from today. But he didn't let on.

"I'll give you a fifty-yard head start and race you to the big willow tree. It's about one hundred fifty yards or one tenth of a klick in military terms. The winner gets what he wants."

"What do you mean, *he* gets what he wants? You're assuming that you'll win. I'm wearing high heels, so that's not fair. We both have to take our shoes off. It's a dirt trail so your toes should be able to stand it."

Sitting down on a large rock, he held out his hands. "Give me your foot."

Emma held up her left leg and John took off her shoe and proceeded to run his hand all the way up to where he nearly touched paradise.

"Take your hand out. You haven't won the race yet." Emma removed her right shoe herself and took off running.

Laughing she yelled, "Remember, you can't run until you take off your Ranger boots."

He watched her as she ran and he thought: I *will* come back to you, and it won't matter if I have to storm the Gates of Hell itself to do it.

"Okay. I gave you a big head start. You better run faster." He lit out after her.

It started to rain. Emma looked back to see John's feet fly straight up as he slipped in the mud on the path. He landed on his back, and when she saw that he wasn't moving, she started to freak out. Running back to him, she cried, "John, say something. Are you hurt?"

He opened his eyes, and looking at Emma with adoration said, "I'm a Ranger, remember?" Putting his hands behind his head, he spoke as a Captain. "Now lean over and give me some mouth-to-mouth resuscitation or I might not make it."

Emma sat in the mud and wiped the grime off his face and began to kiss him passionately thinking: you have no idea how much I love you. She loved his moist lips and those eyes that she thought could see right into her soul.

They lay there in the mud, kissing and fondling each other as the rain began to pour down. Finally, it was too much for them, so they ran to a gazebo to escape the deluge. Sitting down on a bench, John held her close.

Emma began to shiver.

He stood up and took off his shirt, rung the water out and put it around her. "This will help keep you warm." He sat back down and Emma hugged him tight, and as she did, she saw his dog tags again and that made her say another silent prayer to bring him home to her and their unborn child to be.

Finally, the rain stopped and Emma took John's glasses and gently cleaned them with the one part of her dress that didn't have mud on it. Then it dawned on her. "John, I didn't think a soldier could wear glasses if he were in an infantry unit."

"You're right, he can't. These belonged to a friend of mine who was in the quartermaster corps. When he went home he gave them to me, and I had regular glass put in. He told me that they were lucky glasses. I guess he proved his point when that Taliban round knocked them off my face. Ever since then I made it a point to wear them in battle. It made my guys feel like they were protected by some supernatural force."

"But you were wearing them in Athens International Airport."

"That's because, sweetie, when I saw you I thought wearing them might bring me luck with you. In fact you were looking at me when I put them on."

"You devil! That's so deceitful, it's....it's stupid and it won't work."

"It seems to me that it worked because I got in your pants."

"I still can't believe that you would do that in order to get me in the sack."

"It's part two of the Ranger Way: "Do whatever it takes to win.""

She balled a fist. "I'm so furious at you. Just as soon as we get cleaned up I'm going to check the lenses."

"Put them on now. You don't need your machine to check them. After all, you don't wear glasses."

Emma put them on and looked at John. He appeared perfectly clear. "Okay, so you're right. I'm still mad at you."

"Does this mean the wedding is off?"

"No! But I might punish you with no Ranger Way tonight."

"Emma, that's too harsh of a punishment. How about sending me to bed without my supper?"

Digging her fingernails into his bare arm, she said with a scowl on her face, "That won't work. You'll still want your dessert."

He looked down at his arm. "You know, if we were already married, I could turn you in for spousal abuse."

"The judge would throw the case out because he would ask you to swear on the Bible that you were telling the truth, which seems to be a problem for you."

"One thing I never lie about is when I say I'm madly in love with you, and I'm happy that tomorrow you'll be Mrs. John Peterson."

"Me too. I'm looking forward to tomorrow, but I'm going to love that glorious day in a week or so when you come home safe. Let's go home and get cleaned up. Oh, and you're forgiven. Tomorrow is going to be a busy day. We will need to get some sleep. By the way, dear, I guess you can still have your dessert tonight."

John kissed her neck and whispered, "That's just what I wanted to hear."

Sleeping in until 9:00am caused John and Emma to scurry out the door and head to the jewelry store.

After getting the rings they had resized and trying them on, John took out a large stack of bills to pay for them.

"Good lord, John, doesn't the Army pay by check?"

"It depends. This is combat pay. For every day a soldier is on the line he gets hazardous duty or combat pay. It's the Army's way of thanking us for almost getting our asses shot off and for shooting the hell out of the bad guys."

Emma changed the subject. "John, I want you to drop me off at Jane's house. I'll meet you at the church at 1:30. You're already dressed in your uniform, but I want to look really pretty for you."

"You already looked beautiful to me, even when you're covered in mud."

"But today I want to look even prettier."

John tried to kiss her but she covered her mouth. "The next time you kiss me I'll be Mrs. John Peterson."

John left Emma at her sister's and went to meet up with Martin.

Walking up to John, Martin handed a small box to him.

"What is it?"

"See for yourself. It's the Distinguished Service Cross. You forgot it on purpose, didn't you? You deserve the second highest decoration our country can bestow on a soldier. Why the hell don't you want to wear it?"

"Better men deserve it."

"John, what the fuck is the matter with you?"

"I'm not a hero."

"Put it on your damn uniform. Now."

"Okay. I'll wear it. Emma won't know what the DSC is anyway."

"You and I know and Seemans knows, too. So wear it, if not for yourself but for Charlie 2-5. They would want you to. I also have the unit citations that 2-5 won plus your service stars and your purple heart."

"Jesus Christ, Martin, I got bit by a damn snake, remember? Hell, maybe the Army should have given the purple heart to the fucking snake."

John and Martin sat down on a park bench and started throwing rocks and making them skip across the water in a small pond.

"John, remember that time when we were over by that lake outside Kabul and some kids weren't catching any fish and they were really upset?"

"Sure do, Martin. You pulled the pin on a grenade and threw it about forty feet into the lake, and then kaboom! Those kids had all the fish they wanted. God that was funny."

"It looked like it was raining fish, and John, one of them went down in your fatigues and started flopping all around, and man, you started freaking out."

"No wonder. I thought it might be one of those Pacu testicle biting fish. You would've freaked out too. There are stories about guys getting their nuts bitten off."

"Yeah, but John, the way you were pulling your fatigues down was a riot, and the fish turned out to be just a little sun fish. Remember, you offered it to the kids, but since they saw where it came from, none of them wanted it."

As they sat there laughing and reminiscing over their time in Afghanistan, Emma, with Jane and Ellen, was getting dressed for her wedding.

In walked her mother. "Anything I can do to help?"

"Yes, Mom. You can go to the wedding."

"I mean now."

"No. You can stay, but I don't want any advice. You've already made it clear that you're disappointed that John's not a Catholic. I didn't want to have to tell you this, Mom, but John is a Muslim."

"What?" Carol shouted.

While fixing Emma's hair, Jane spoke up and looked at her mother. "Emma is just kidding, Mom, so you don't need to get upset."

Ellen said, "I can vouch for that since he is my brother, although he might be leaning toward becoming a Hare Krishna."

"So you see, Mom, things could be worse."

This brought a chuckle from Carol.

"How do I look?"

"You're wearing a Vince Camuto Crepe A-Line dress? I do like the Jessica Simpson Claudette Pump, but a pale blue dress and dark blue shoes? I thought you would have chosen white."

Emma, looking perturbed, said, "You thought wrong, Mother. I'm marrying a soldier, not a prince. Clothing from Nordstrom's is good enough for me. I got everything for less than $500.00. Aren't you the one who said I should be frugal? Well, I took your advice. You should be proud of me."

Carol went over and hugged Emma and looked into her eyes. "I *am* proud of you, honey, and I think you're getting a wonderful man and he's getting a beautiful woman." Carol wiped tears from her eyes. "Let me hug my beautiful daughter one more time before she is married. I like your one strand of pearls and the pale blue nail polish."

Ellen looked at her watch. "We'd better get going to the church."

***

As the car rounded the corner, they saw a crowd of people waiting on the lawn outside The Sacred Heart of Jesus Catholic Church.

Ellen said, "I wonder what's going on?"

Emma noticed that Carol was looking away from her, as if she didn't want to make eye contact.

"What did you do, Mother?"

"I only mentioned the wedding to Peggy Madonna at Fox News, but I didn't know this would happen."

"Well, it did." She sighed. "I guess it's okay. There are a lot of Rangers here so I assume they're from John's company."

They got out of the car and were immediately congratulated by the Rangers and their wives.

Walking over to Emma, Peggy Madonna waved a microphone at her. "Emma, you look absolutely stunning in that outfit. Soon you'll be Mrs. John Peterson. Do you have anything to say to our Colorado television audience?"

She spoke into the microphone. "This is the happiest day of my life."

Someone in the crowd yelled, "Let's hear it for Captain

Peterson and his bride."

"Hooah, hooah, hooah, hooah, hooah!"

"This is Peggy Madonna reporting from Boulder."

Emma, Ellen, Jane and Carol went into the bride's room as Father Pierce walked up to the altar with a big grin on his face. As he looked at the now almost filled church, he heard a voice say, "Attention all ranks. General officer is in the building. I mean church."

As General Seemans and JoAnn walked down the aisle, smiling at everyone, General Seemans said, "Please, everyone, take your seats. I must apologize for my overly enthusiastic officer."

As John walked up to the pulpit, he reached out and shook the Father's hand. Standing there in his new Captain's uniform with a spit shine on his black shoes and all his medals and service stars on the left side of his chest, his silver wings right under them centered, signifying that he was an airborne Ranger, he turned to the filled pews and stood straight up at parade rest. His feet were twelve inches apart and his arms were behind him with his right hand overlapping his left hand, in the center of his back, and his thumbs formed an "X". It was regulations. John stood there for a few minutes, listening to the organ music and then the music changed to *Ave Maria*. He thought: that's the music they play at funerals. Come to think of it, I guess it's okay. He then saw Martin and Jane walking down the aisle, looking right at him. After them came Maggie throwing rose petals in all directions. Then everyone stood up and turned and looked at

Emma with her hand on her father's arm as they walked down the aisle. John's and Emma's gazes locked on to each other.

Emma thought: there is my beloved—the man that God made for me.

John thought: I'm going to have a great time tonight, even better than the previous nights, and I'm damn lucky she'll soon by my wife.

Now taking communion, Emma whispered to John, "Dear, there's a General looking right at you, so don't try to chicken out, or he'll have you shot."

He whispered back, "Not a chance, honey, not a chance."

After what seemed like an eternity, Father Pierce got down to the only part of the ceremony that really mattered: "John, do you take Emma to be your lawful wedded wife, to have and to hold, and to be faithful to her until death do you part?"

As John answered, "I Do" he said a prayer for Emma. *God, if you're listening, for Emma's sake more than mine, please don't let me wind up coming home in a casket.*

"Emma, do you take John to be your lawful wedded husband, to have and to hold, and to be faithful to him until death do you part?"

As Emma answered, "I Do" she prayed, *Bring him home safely to me, lord.*

After their rings were exchanged, Father Pierce said, "You may kiss your bride."

John took Emma in his arms and softly pressed his lips to hers. Then they turned and looked to the crowd as Father Pierce said, "I now present to you Captain and Mrs. John Peterson."

Everyone gave them a standing ovation, but what was on the minds of all the Rangers was that they knew, in less than a week, they'd be called on to unleash hell on the Taliban. Emma still didn't know everything. It was just as well that she didn't know. She was entitled to have a few happy hours with her husband and lover.

As John and a beaming Emma walked down the aisle, she noticed all John's fellow officers were gone, and only their wives were still seated. As they got to the door of the church, Tenny pushed it open, and Emma was astonished to see that the officers had formed two lines for them to walk between.

Tenny said, "Officers, draw your swords." They formed an arch of swords for Captain Peterson and Mrs. Peterson to walk under.

Emma smiled and said to John, "This is wonderful."

Martin said to John and Emma, "With your permission, Captain, we would like for you and the beautiful Emma to board our mode of transportation on this happy occasion, which just happens to be an Army Humvee. As you can see, sir, it comes equipped with a fifty caliber machinegun, which I'm sure Emma will be glad to use on you if you get too drunk at our next destination."

"Martin, how did you get the Humvee?"

"Compliments of General Seemans."

Emma asked, "Where are we going now?"

"To Bivouac for mess, Mrs. Peterson."

As John helped Emma into the Humvee, she looked puzzled. "John, what does that mean?"

"They are taking us somewhere for our wedding reception."

"Did you know about this?"

"No."

Following behind a military escort, they soon found themselves outside *The Blue Parrot Restaurant* in Louisville.

"How would they know that we like this place unless someone had told them?"

"I don't know. You can ask Martin. He's the one in Army Intelligence."

Gripping his hand and kissing him on his neck, she said, "I know you told him. I can tell when you're lying...it's when you say anything."

Their entourage took up the entire patio seating, which held all of Charlie 2-5 and their wives. At the head table sat John and Emma, and on John's side were Lieutenants Martin, Peoples, Gee, and Sergeant Major Tennyson, and on Emma's side were their wives, Betty, Ann, Lynn, and Mary Jo.

The weather was perfect, unlike what Charlie 2-5 would be facing in a few days. There wouldn't be any laughing and drinking then, only killing and hopefully rescuing their Rangers.

Everyone had the same dinner, which consisted of a salad, spaghetti, meatballs and sausage, and raviolis. The drinks ranged from beer to bourbon. There was wine for everybody for the toast. Emma looked around and saw that everyone had the same dinner. She asked Betty if that was to save money?

All four women said, "Army regulations."

As Emma laughed with them, John told the waiter, "Bring Emma a Vodka Martini."

Emma told John "I don't need one anymore. This isn't Chicago. You don't need to get me drunk to get what you want, sweetie. Besides my drinking days are over now."

"Are you going on the wagon, honey?"

"Yes, for nine months." She rubbed her flat stomach.

"Oh, yeah. I didn't think about that."

Betty had heard what Emma said and told all of the ladies. They promptly started telling her what she could look forward to.

Then two waiters brought out the cake. The cake was not white or chocolate but a khakis color with *John and Emma* stenciled on the top of it in red frosting letters.

After the cake was eaten, the toasts were next.

General Seemans and JoAnn were sitting at a table with John and Emma's parents and Father Pierce. General Seemans stood to make the first toast. "John, it's been known since George Washington was a General that no one ever wanted to get on the wrong side of the General. Well, Captain Peterson, I'm going to let you in on a little secret. What's worse is getting on the wrong side of your wife. This is far worse than having a General on your case. The

General will forget what you did. The wife will never forget."

JoAnn stood up. "That's not true, John. A wife only remembers ninety-five percent of the things she didn't like."

Everybody laughed—they figured that they had better laugh.

Finally, after about three hours, the party began to break up, and John and Emma got into a limo that took them back to Emma's house where they collected the clothes they'd need, and then they drove down to the Broadmoor Hotel for two nights, thanks to Charlie 2-5.

They didn't speak much on the drive down to the Broadmoor. It was really starting to sink in that, in a week, they'd be happy or unhappy, depending if John got injured or worse. Emma didn't want to think about that. She just kept saying a prayer to God over and over.

John, knowing what he would be facing, kept going over in his mind the plan to rescue his men, keep his Rangers alive, and get back home to Emma.

He glanced at her. "Wow, we're going to have a baby. I'll be a dad next year. I wonder what we'll be doing then. You'll be running your practice and changing diapers, and me and my buddies will be running our *Steel Protection Group*."

"You're right, honey, only you'll be changing diapers, too. We can take turns washing them."

"Haven't you heard of throw away diapers?"

"We're not using them, John. They're bad for the

environment."

At the Broadmoor, they went to bed and looked out the window at the stars.

John snuggled up close to Emma, their naked bodies touching, warm flesh on warm flesh, from their heads to their toes. "I wonder if there's any life among the stars up there," John mused. "Assuming there's intelligent life out there, I wonder if they've spent the better part of their existence trying to murder each other. Maybe it's just an earthling thing."

"I hope it is. I wouldn't wish war on anybody anywhere in the universe."

"Emma, we only have until Monday at fourteen-hundred hours, and then I have to report in and get my platoon ready to go. You and the other wives can come to the field at two-hundred hours to see us off, but as God is my witness, we *will* be back no later than a week from tomorrow, and I *will* be back to stay."

Without lifting her head, she said, "I hope so."

"We've had a few ups and downs, but the downs weren't all that bad, and the ups were unbelievable, and still are. I want you to keep telling yourself that this will be over soon, and we'll never be parted again."

With her tears running down his chest, she took the bed sheet and wiped them off. Trying to think what to say, all she could come up with was, "I love you and I think I did when I first saw you in McDonald's. I've heard of love at first sight but I didn't really believe it would happen to me. Was it love at first sight for you?"

"Yeah, it was. I thought it might be hopeless but then, with each thing that happened, I began to hope we could be together. Today it all came to fruition. Whatever you see on the news, don't let it worry you. I *will* come back. We're dealing with a murderous bunch of cutthroats who can terrorize the locals but not us. We'll be going in with the Air Force providing air support and backed up by five companies of Rangers with a decoy attack plan that those dumb sons of bitches will take hook, line, and sinker. Baby, they won't know what hit them, and it'll be over very quickly."

Emma took a deep breath. "I believe you, John. I have no other choice."

"Emma, I am kind of hungry. How about we get some room service? I could use a steak. How about you?"

"Well, I wouldn't mind a salad, but no raw steak. If I started eating like you, I might give birth to a zombie instead of a beautiful baby. I'm going to start eating some organ foods like liver because it is very good for our baby."

With that cute smile on his face that she loved, John took her in his arms, and standing at the foot of the bed, held her naked body, and giving her a little peck of a kiss, he said, "Liver? The last time I checked, liver was meat. Are you pulling a one-eighty on me?"

"No. I'm not going to eat liver because I like it, but because it's necessary. I'll be doing other things too. A friend of mine is a dietitian, and she'll make up menus for me that'll include fatty acids because they aid in brain and eye development. I have an appointment with my OB/GYN for Wednesday, and then I'll be seeing her once a month after that."

"I'll say one thing, sweetie, you're very efficient."

Annoyed over his one-eighty line, she said, "John, order our food and put some clothes on."

"You too, honey."

As they ate their food, Emma turned on the CNN news. She was sorry she did. They were running a special on the White Fox from a feed on Al Jazeera television out of Saudi Arabia. He was bragging about how he would personally preside over the executions of the three Rangers.

He paraded them before the cameras and tried to get them to confess their crimes against Islam. They wouldn't. Corporal Pepper did say, "Hay Foxy! Captain Peterson will personally blow your goddamn head clean off, and that, shit head, you can count on."

The live feed then went dead.

John became enraged. Emma watched and said nothing.

John walked around with his fists clenched so tightly that his knuckles were solid white, and grumbling in a low voice said, "I'm going to kill that fucking prick. Now I can't wait to get over there. We're going to kill them all. Every damn one of those sons of bitches!"

Glancing at a frightened Emma, John cooled down. "Sorry, sugar. Why don't we go for a walk? It's a nice night."

Knowing how John was hurting over his missing men, Emma, still a little shaken by his outrage and with a solemn look on her face, nodded while staring in his eyes. "That's a very good idea. There's an ice cream store down the block. I wouldn't mind an ice cream cone and maybe a pickle."

"A pickle?"

"There's an old wives' tale that pregnant women have a craving for ice cream and pickles. I guess, John, I'll find out pretty soon if it's true."

"No kidding. I've never heard of that before."

"Have you been living under a rock?"

Walking hand in hand and swinging them back and forth, they used their free hands to hold their ice cream cones. Emma's was BaseBall Nut while John had opted for Mint Chocolate Chip.

"Emma, on this date next year I want the three of us to come back here and do what we're doing now. Our baby will love Mint Chocolate Chip."

Emma agreed but with one exception: "Our baby will want BaseBall Nut. On second thought, it'll be Mint Chocolate Chip. Our baby might choke on the nuts. You were right, dear."

The two of them stopped on a small bridge spanning a small creek. They looked down at the water that glistened from time to time, a reflection of a streetlight. They licked their ice cream cones and listened to the sound the water made as it rushed by.

Then they heard a cell phone ring. It was John's.

"Yes, this is Captain Peterson." He said nothing for a minute. "I understand completely the necessity for the change, General. Tomorrow at eleven-hundred hours. Yes, sir. I'll see you then, sir."

John took one last lick of Mint Chocolate Chip and then dropped the cone in the water and watched it disappear downstream.

Dread filled Emma's stomach. "You're leaving tomorrow, John?"

"Tuesday morning at four-hundred hours." John walked Emma back to the hotel. "This is a tough way to start a marriage. I feel like I've done you a terrible disservice. When I get back, I'll make it up to you every day for the rest of my life."

"John, you didn't ask for this. I know things will be okay. God didn't let us find each other for just a few weeks and then nothing. You'll come back to me, safe and sound. I know it. Hugging his arm she added, "Besides, you have your lucky glasses."

***

Getting up on a beautiful Sunday morning, John and Emma ate their breakfast in the hotel dining room and then made the drive back to Fort Carson.

"You know, Emma, I looked around the dining room and thought how lucky all of the other hotel guests are. They aren't worried about where they'll be in forty-eight hours. This will be all over for us soon, and then me and my buddies will let somebody else put their butts on the line. Maybe they should bring back the draft. If they ever did, there'd be a human cry so loud you could hear it on Mars. I've had a belly full of war."

"John, I'm so glad you said that. I don't see how the wives of career soldiers can stand the living hell of never knowing whether their husbands will come home alive from their latest deployment."

"Emma, honey, the odds are in our favor. On the other hand, the life expectancy of a Taliban insurgent from the time he takes to the field against us is a little over three months."

"Good grief! It seems like they wouldn't have anybody joining up."

"They get lots of recruits because they are ignorant as hell. Their leaders aren't putting their necks on the line. They're too smart for that. I killed the White Fox's kid because he was in the wrong place at the right time."

Pulling up in front of John's quarters, he told Emma, "Wear something really pretty because at nineteen-hundred we'll be going to the sendoff party for 2-5. There'll be food and a lot of booze and dancing."

They went inside, and John immediately took a shower. As he washed his hair with his eyes closed, he heard the shower door open and soon felt Emma's hands rubbing his back. He started to say something, but she said, "Shush." She got down on her knees and rubbed his butt and legs with her soapy hands. "Turn around and stand at attention and do what I say or you'll be busted to a Major or something."

John turned and faced Emma, laughing, his eyes still closed. "Busted to a Major, huh? Well, that would be one rank up from a Captain, so that sounds pretty good."

She soaped him up good.

"Oh, oh, Emma, you really know your stuff. Standing at attention never felt like this before. I can only imagine what parade rest would feel like."

"Sweetie, give it a try and see if it is any better."

At parade rest, John groaned. "It's about the same and it's wonderful. I'm promoting you to...*gasp*...Sergeant in charge of the shower."

She kept rubbing him with her soapy hands.

Barely able to speak, he managed, "Oh, promotion is effective immediately." He moaned. His knees almost buckled as his body shook with pleasure.

"I'm happy to see you like my sendoff party for you."

Taking Emma by her hands, he pulled her up to eye level. "This was the best shower I've ever had. Thank you, honey. When I get back next week we should practice this some more. It's a big incentive to rescue my men and shoot the hell out of the bad guys in a hurry!"

Emma kissed him. "John, I'll be waiting with bated breath. Now, using an Army term, you better get your ass in gear, or you'll be late for your appointment with General Seemans."

"Okay. Where did you hear that expression?"

"I heard some Sergeant yelling that to some soldiers the other day, and he sounded really mad."

"He was probably putting on an act to drive home a point to recruits." John dried off and then dressed regulation for his meeting with General Seemans.

Kissing Emma goodbye, John got a Jeep from motor pool and drove over to Regimental Headquarters. He met Martin and they went in together.

"John, how was the Broadmoor?"

"It was great. I'm sorry our stay was cut short. Martin, we have to make this a surgical assault, kill those assholes, get our guys, and get our asses back to Carson. I don't think we'll be hearing any bullshit about shooting only at designated targets."

"One thing you're going to hear, John, is that we are to capture White Fox and kill him only if our own lives are in danger."

"You're probably right, Martin. But we can get around those orders by saying that we don't know where the round came from that killed him."

"It's true, John, soldiers have been using that line of crap forever. Hell, it probably originated in Vietnam. Fuckin' rules of engagement. The problem is that the Brass has heard it too."

"Yeah, but any two-star who'd question us would more than likely have been a line officer himself, and he knows what it's like to be under enemy fire with rounds coming from all directions. So the bottom line is he'll just look the other way and stuff the White Fox's death under the table."

"John, you really want to kill this guy that bad?"

"Hell yes, I do!"

***

Back at John's officer's quarters, Emma was cleaning up the place so that it would be easy to vacate the quarters when John got back and mustered out of the service. She heard a knock on the door. It was Betty and Ann.

"Come on in, girls."

Betty said, "We want to invite you to our nightly prayer service. It's open to all the wives of 2-5. This is the last tour for all of them. It's against Army regulations for any soldier to serve more than three tours in a war zone. Plus our sweeties are getting out and going into the weed protection business."

"Oh, my God, that means Larry will come home, smelling like Marijuana," Ann exclaimed.

Mary Jo, who had just arrived, said, "That beats the gun powder that I've smelled the last twenty years."

***

John and Martin walked out of the meeting, griping to each other. Martin said, "See you tonight, John, this was a waste of four hours. Hell, as soon as the first round is fired, the battle plan goes out the window. Everybody knows that except the geniuses in the

Pentagon."

"See you then, Martin."

Emma, seeing him coming, opened the door "I better not ask how it went because if you told me you'd have to kill me because it's a secret."

"Actually, Emma, their plan is like every other one that they have come up with in the last three years. It's a joke. We'll do whatever it takes to get our Rangers back. The Pentagon is more interested in getting the White Fox. They made our men's rescue secondary. It doesn't matter. We're the ones with boots on the ground, not them. Let's talk about something else. You haven't been at your office much. Do you have worked stacked up?"

"Well, I see where your soldier is coming back to see me. I talked to Rich, and he was able to get the drug, so your soldier is already showing improvement. Then there's Mary Cottonwood. She has a cataract that she needs to have removed. It's a simple procedure, but she is freaking out over it. Like a lot of people nowadays, she went online and read up on cataracts and also read the baloney that people post. So I know she's coming to see me so that I can reassure her for the tenth time. In a couple of weeks, she'll be back for the eleventh time. My mother left me an email. She wants to know how things are going and did we go to church. I wrote back that we're too busy screwing to attend church."

"No you didn't!"

"No, I didn't but I should have. You just missed the girls. We're going to get together every day until you all return safely."

"The prayer thing."

"Exactly."

"Add this to the prayer. *Praise the Lord and pass the ammunition.* It could come in handy."

"John, I do believe in God. I'll pray for you in earnest daily until you come home safe, and then I'll thank God again and again every day for the rest of my life."

John showered again but not with Emma this time. She waited until he was out of the bathroom before she came in for her shower.

"I thought you would join me?"

"Sorry, honey, one per day. That's regulations."

"That's not Army regulations."

"It is now."

***

Upon arriving at the sendoff party at exactly nineteen-hundred hours, John and Emma were surprised to see everyone looking glum. John walked over to Martin. "What's going on?"

"Five minutes ago the time was moved up again. A few of us are hanging out to make sure everyone gets the word. The bus picks us up at two-hundred hours. Liftoff is three-hundred hours."

Taking Emma's hand, he had to pull her because he was walking so fast. Before he opened the car door, he said, "Maybe this is a blessing in disguise. The quicker we get the battle over with, the sooner I come back to you."

"John, if you really want to make love again that would be okay."

"No, Emma. Let me get my fatigues and combat boots on. Then let's wait out the time on the porch."

They sat in lawn chairs, watching the Air Force transport being loaded with all their gear.

Then everything began to hit home with Emma. She thought: this is like being on death row, waiting to be executed. They had only known each other for such a short period of time and had fallen in love. "John, we don't deserve this. This is awful. If you weren't getting out of the Army, I wouldn't be married to you. If this isn't hell on earth then I don't know what is. I'm beginning to hate three soldiers I've never met because they may have ruined our lives and the life of our baby. You shouldn't have volunteered to go back. What happens if you die? Is that miserable country worth dying for? I don't think so. What would happen if you told them you changed your mind and won't go?"

"Nothing would happen. My enlistment was technically up two days ago. It was for all of us, kind of a reward from the Army. It wouldn't have mattered anyway. We have to get our men back."

"What? I thought you had six weeks left. You lied to me again. Were you lying just to get me to marry you? What does that stupid Ranger Way thing really mean anyhow? Is that just a line you Rangers use to get some bimbo to spread her legs? Maybe that's all I really am to you...just a bimbo."

"No you're not. I really love you and I always will."

His cell rang again. "Yes, sir, I understand. I'll leave right now." He hung up. "Emma, I have to go over some last minute details. I hope to see you at the field. If not I'll see you in less than a week."

"Maybe I'll be at the field. I honestly don't know."

He made no attempt to kiss her. He just said softly, "I really love you. The days we have had together were the most wonderful days of my life. See you soon." Then he left.

Emma sat there watching it get darker and darker and saw a plane flying by, playing hide and go seek with the clouds. She looked up at the stars and remembered how she and John had talked about them.

Finally, with only thirty minutes to go before they were to leave, Emma got in her car to drive to the field. She had a flat tire. She panicked and drove slowly with the car clunking along at twenty miles an hour. She made it to the chain-link fence with only minutes to spare. She saw John talking to his officers. She yelled as loud as she could. He didn't hear her, but one of his Rangers did. He ran over to John and pointed at Emma. John ran to her as fast as he could.

With her fingers sticking in through the fence, she pulled her face up as close as she could get. Crying profusely she said, "I'm so sorry. You have to come back to me or I'll die."

John put his lips up to the fence and they kissed each other through the chain links. "Emma, take care of our baby. I'll be back. I have to go. Love you forever."

She watched John run and catch up with the last of Charlie 2-5 boarding the plane. Now all alone, she sank down to the ground and leaned her head on the fence and just stayed there until dawn.

After getting the tire fixed, she cleaned out his quarters. It was then that she saw his lucky glasses on the nightstand. He must've forgotten them because she was selfish and mean to him.

Emma drove back to Boulder, stopping five times on the road to cry. Knowing that it would take another eleven hours for John to get to Afghanistan, she closed her office for the day and went home to get some sleep. She got some rest but very little sleep. The next morning she went to her office and was immediately confronted by an irate Mary Cottonwood, a plump woman in her fifties who never had a kind word to say to Emma.

"Doctor Peterson, I want you to tell me the truth about my eyes and I mean now."

"I'll tell you the truth, Mary. I saw my husband, Captain John Peterson, leave yesterday morning and go to war for people like you. I can only pray to God that he comes home alive and well. As far as your eyes go, they can easily be fixed, Mary. What no doctor can fix is that disgusting, ME FIRST attitude of yours. Now get out of my office before I call the police."

A sheepish looking Mary turned and looked back at a very upset Emma.

Emma screamed, "Get out." She then picked up her cell phone and went into her office and sat down and looked at a selfie she had taken of her and John while they were lying on the broken bed in his officer's quarters. Then exhausted, she lay her head down on her desk and went to sleep, having no idea what was happening 8,000 miles away.

***

Now over their drop zone, John told his men to prepare to jump. "It's time. In unison, boys, now what do we say as we jump?"

"When I get to Heaven

to Saint Peter I will tell,

another Ranger reporting, sir,

I served my time in Hell."

Soon the night sky was filled with black parachutes and the men wearing those parachutes had only one thing on their minds: survive.

Charlie 2-5 stalked through three-foot-tall grass, and then through a swampy area in eighteen inches of water and more grass. Crouching down in the water, they saw two Taliban soldiers with two donkeys loaded down with sticks for firewood. This gave John an idea.

He whispered to Lieutenant Peoples, "Larry, get a couple of our boys to take them out. No noise. Cut their damn throats. I want to use the donkeys and the firewood."

***

Back in Boulder, Emma woke up to the sound of her cell. It was Jane inviting her to come over to her house.

Instead, Emma invited Jane to come to her office. She did.

"My God, Emma, you're a mess."

In a soft and solemn tone and with a forlorn look on her face, she replied, "He's over there now and in danger. I can sense it."

Reaching over and hugging Emma, Jane said, "He's going to come home safe. Within a week, you two will be together and this stressful time will soon be long forgotten."

"John has to come home. He just has to or I'll die."

"Emma, don't say that. He'll come home safe. You have to believe that or you'll go insane."

***

John was thinking of Emma just as she was thinking of him. He had his Rangers positioned on three sides of the town. The only way the Taliban could escape was to the south toward the Pakistan border.

Now Charlie 2-5 had to just wait. John sent a message to his men: "Don't fire until our snipers open up first."

At four-fifty hours, the rising sun's rays were shinning right into the eyes of the executioners. The Taliban, having no clue that the Rangers were close by, were berating the three Rangers for the cameras. Finally the three executioners were ready to begin their deadly work. They stood behind the three Rangers and held up big knives.

Little did they know the three of them were in the crosshairs of three of the deadliest snipers in the world. At the same time, the donkeys with their load of wood and their handlers stopped to watch the executions. The three Taliban executioners looked to the White Fox to give them the signal to proceed with the murders.

He nodded his ugly, hairy head.

Before they could do their deadly work, all three of them lay dead behind the Rangers. Each one had been killed by a round to his head from one hundred fifty yards away. Then all hell broke loose.

Two Rangers, now dressed as Taliban insurgents, were standing by the donkeys. They instantly pulled two 30-caliber machineguns from the sticks on the donkeys and began to rake the Taliban with murderous fire. The Taliban terrorists scattered in all directions only to run into fire on three sides from Charlie 2-5 and from three helicopter gunships swooping in from the south.

It was all over in five minutes. There was only one man left standing, the White Fox. He made a run for the buildings.

The three Rangers with their blindfolds still on had no clue as to what had just transpired until they heard a voice say, "Has anybody seen any dumbass Rangers around here who want to go home?"

Ogden yelled, "It's Captain Peterson! I knew 2-5 wouldn't abandon us."

Leaving Tenny to untie the Rangers, John and Martin went

looking for the White Fox. Searching building after building, they came down to the last one in the town. John entered it first with Martin close behind. As John cautiously went into the last room, he saw something out the corner of his eye. He turned and fired and put ten rounds into a full length mirror.

Martin slapped John on the back and laughed. "Well, I'll be damned, a modern-day Billy the Kid just beat himself to the draw."

John looked at Martin with a sly smile. "Shut the fuck up. You better not tell any of my men what happened. I'd never live this down."

As they walked out of the building, Lieutenant Peoples walked up with a very smelly White Fox. "I found him hiding under the floor of a latrine."

Charlie 2-5 began to egress the town with their one prisoner. The first group was taken out by the helicopters, leaving the third platoon and John and Martin to be extracted later. The helicopters would soon return for them. It was then that a sandstorm suddenly came up from the west. At the same time, a large force of Taliban insurgents came up from the south. John had his men form a perimeter with woods on both sides of them and a small stream in front of them.

It was then that the sandstorm let up and John saw that an overwhelming force was in front of him and the third platoon.

The Taliban came across the stream very slowly only to be cut down by Charlie 2-5. But wave after wave of them kept coming.

John looked at Martin, and they both thought the same thing. They were running out of ammunition. Everyone in the third platoon knew that their lives were almost over. They all pulled out their last hand grenades. They would wait until the enemy was on them, and only then would they grip the handle and pull the safety pin then drop the grenades as they were dying.

All of 2-5 were thinking about their homes and loved ones.

It was then, in desperation, with bullets flying in every direction, that John called Fox one zero. Acting as his own Forward Observer he radioed, "Fox one zero. This is Charlie E-nine. Request fire, over."

"Charlie E-nine, this is Fox one zero. What are your coordinates?"

"Fox one zero, adjust your fire to one-zero-zero."

"Charlie E-nine, this is Fox one zero. If we fire on one-zero-zero, we'll be firing on your position."

"That is affirmative. Change the coordinates and fire for effect. Do it now."

"Charlie E-nine, this is Fox one zero, repeat the order."

"Fox one zero. This is Charlie E-nine. Fire for effect, one-zero-zero." John tossed down the radio and fired his last rounds into the hoard of attackers. Two Taliban leapt over the wall. He smashed one in the face with the butt of useless rifle then drew his knife and cut the other bastard's throat. Three more came over the wall. Martin pumped the last of his bullets into them.

As the artillery shells rained down, John dove for cover. Cordite and dirt blew through the air. He looked at Emma's picture on his cell phone and sent her a text message: "I will love you forever, take good care of our baby."

***

Back in the states, a despondent Emma sat in her office with the lights out and holding John's lucky glasses. On her computer she kept playing the same song in a loop. It was their song: *Will You Still Love Me Tomorrow?* She didn't hear a message chime in on her phone. All she could do was keep saying the same prayer over and over and holding his glasses tighter and tighter.

"God, why have you forsaken me?" She decided to go to the church where she was married and pray for John there. But first she played the song one more time.

Finally, she stood up and walked through her dark and silent office and locked the door and walked down the street to her church. Pulling open the front door, she thought of all the times she had come to pray. She thought of Father Pierce, a perfect wedding and the arch of swords. This time she was here to pray for her husband and her baby.

In the empty church, Emma went to the second row of pews from the front and knelt down. "Hail Mary, full of grace..."

***

Thousands of miles away, the prayer that she was saying to herself, Martin was whispering, and John was listening: "Hail Mary, full of grace, the Lord is with you." The rest of the prayer was drowned out by the shells exploding all around them. John, with his face in the dirt, turned his head to the side and looked at Martin.

Martin was looking at him. "It's been an honor to serve with you, Captain." He pulled the pin on his grenade.

"Likewise." John did the same.

***

Emma, walking with her head bowed, went back toward her office. She heard some men talking on a street corner.

"Man, it took some balls to do what those Rangers did, but they got the White Fox."

"Do they know if any of our guys were killed?"

"The Army hasn't said one way or the other."

Upon hearing that, Emma knew the mission was over. She ran crying back to her office. Now sitting in the dark, she checked her messages and saw the one from John. She read it over and over, and then in utter despair, reached the conclusion that he was telling her "Goodbye."

Around 1:40am, she heard a pounding on the door. She went to see who it was. General Seemans and his wife JoAnn were standing at her door. She was sure they were the bearers of bad news, opened the door, and before the General could say anything, she demanded to know, "How did he die?"

General Seemans smiled. "What? John isn't dead. None of them even received so much as a scratch. They rescued the Rangers and captured the White Fox. For the bravery your Captain Peterson showed, I'm recommending him for the Medal of Honor. Charlie 2-5 is en route home at this very minute. They're over Kansas right now. Emma, I thought you knew. It was all over the television channels. Your sister said you were here. We came by to take you to the field to welcome John and Charlie 2-5 back home."

With that happy news, Emma practically went limp. JoAnn hugged her and she began to cry again.

At 4:55am, as the dawn began to break, a smiling Emma stood in the same spot where she had been sobbing just days before and saw her John march down the ramp of the plane. His uniform was torn and dusty and his face was dirty black. He never looked more beautiful. Her heart jumped with joy. All the wives rushed past the Military Police and ran onto the field. Emma ran up to John, threw her arms around his neck, and kissed him and kissed him and kissed him.

"Emma, I told you I'd be back. What's all the fuss?"

With a big smile and laughing, she said, "You forgot your lucky glasses."

Kissing and hugging her and looking into her adoring eyes, he said, "I don't need them anymore. I have all the luck I'll ever need in this world. I have you."

Emma wiped tears from her eyes on his shoulder. "I have you and our baby and that's all I'll ever want."

The sun rose brightly on the first day of the rest of their lives.

I sent my brave young Rangers to war and they were forged in the blast furnace of battle and tempered in the blood of America's enemies and they came out steel.

Author Unknown

About the Author

George S. Naas is a long-time Colorado resident who owns Golden Publishing Company and writes in a variety of genres. He's an ancient history buff and a romantic at heart. When he's not writing or working, he enjoys bowling and cross-fit. He lives in Lakewood with his wife Dana.

Look for other novels by George S. Naas

Invasion of the Lesbian Zombies

Abused and humiliated by men, Brenda goes on a quest for beauty and revenge that leads to her death on an operating table in Haiti, but with the help of a Voodoo High Priestess and Loa the Lesbian Goddess of the Universe, she's brought back from the dead with a mission to empower all women, recruit other beauties into her lesbian sisterhood, and destroy the men who've done them wrong.

Buy from Amazon: https://www.amazon.com/dp/0692135642

Anything Goes

FBI Agent Brad Tillman and hostage negotiator Dr. Joyce Taylor pit their investigative and psychological skills against a homicidal-maniac determined to kill everyone he feels is responsible for the deaths of his wife, daughter, and son. The cat and mouse case involves broken promises, outright lies, and a deadly game of nuclear Russian roulette, as five suitcase nukes are set to go off around the country, two of which are fakes, but which two, and who is next to die?

Buy from Amazon: https://www.amazon.com/dp/B01FGUS9TW

God's Assassin

This is the story of two brothers, Horus and Seth, both gods of ancient Egypt. Horus is an assassin for the Eternal, Lord of Hosts, killing evil people in the name of justice. Seth is the greatest evil the world has ever known. 3500 years ago, Horus, unwilling to kill his brother, imprisoned him in a tomb to save the world from his tyrannical rule. Now the walls are crumbling, and soon, good and evil will clash in the final battle of Armageddon. Caught in the middle is an American family who will play a vital role in the fate of the world.

Buy from Amazon: http://www.amazon.com/dp/B00COW2O3I

Charlie the Cherry

This is a children's (ages 4-6) picture book that tells the story of the trials and tribulations of the last cherry on the cherry tree and how his faith helps him to become a new cherry tree.

Buy from Amazon: https://www.amazon.com/dp/B0155R5IAE